Kill Team

Kill Series – Book Two

Richard A. Powell II

KILL TEAM

ISBN: 0692070915

ISBN-13: 978-0692070918

ACKNOWLEDGEMENTS

I just want to acknowledge all the great storytellers that have and continue to influence and inspire me. I try to do my own thing, for better or for worse, but I can't help but allow the masters of story to inhabit my brain and work their magic.

So, thank you - Kurt Vonnegut, Jr., Stephen King, Damon Lindelof, Chuck Palahniuk, Christopher Nolan, Gillian Flynn, Quentin Tarantino, Jeremy Robert Johnson, & Mark Z. Danielewski.

www.richardapowellii.com

Other works by Richard A. Powell II:

Kill Academy: Kill Series - Book One (2017)
RejectGuy99 (2015)
A Room Full of Keys (2013)
Neither Snow, Nor Rain, Nor Zombie
Infection & Other Strange Tales (2012)

Available by order at bookstores and online
worldwide

Richard A. Powell II

1

There are a million and one ways to kill a person. Guns, knives, chemicals, drowning, and choking. Each one of those has hundreds of subsets. Grenades, bombs, and RPG launchers can do the trick. A vehicle is a hell of a deadly weapon too. Fire, ice, concrete, tar pits, and burying someone alive in good old-fashioned dirt are also among the many techniques.

As a contract assassin, I can use a bevy of nearly unlimited ways to take out a hard target. Granted, the contract itself may offer some guidelines or restrictions as to how the death must appear (or not appear). Discounting that, my line of work can allow for a certain degree of creative expression, which can be nice. I know, that sounds a bit crass, but it is what it is. I don't sell bouquets carefully assembled to order in a corner shop near the business district. I kill people ... for money ... and that, in and of itself, is a crass thing, so discussing it in such a manner is of no consequence to me.

My latest mission on the Kill Team, for which I am Point this time around, has allowed me little discretion in the technique department. This guy, one Mercurio Sharpe, must end up dead by any means necessary. On the surface, that felt ripe with opportunities. After three weeks' worth of recon, however, it became clear my options are going to be limited, mostly because this guy rarely leaves his sanctuary anymore -

a now defunct single-story brick building that once housed a seedy strip club. Another issue is that he's always surrounded by a dozen people. My guess - he understands the stakes and knows he's in danger.

Mercurio is on the verge of ratting out a fellow underground competitor in the counterfeit merchandise game. In the eastern half of the United States, twenty-two percent of the counterfeit merchandise coming in from China are from his efforts. Another twenty percent comes from a competitor in Florida. The federal government put the squeeze on both of them despite not having enough evidence to nab either one. Mercurio caved. In exchange for some physical evidence and testimony against the Florida operation, the government offered Mercurio a two-year blind eye on his own dealings. They must have believed getting one organization broken down was better than none.

The problem is, the Florida syndicate got wind of it, so here we are. When we received the contract, it was my turn to take the lead. On our last mission, Vick was Point but I wish I had been. Suicide. That is what the contract required. It must look like a suicide. At first glance, that sounded like a heavy constraint, and in some ways, it was, however, I could think of many ways people kill themselves. The city where the mission took place helped Vick make the decision. Pittsburgh, the city of three rivers. Rivers meant bridges. He had fun with that one. Lucky bastard. He found a quiet moment in the middle of the night to lure Joseph Francis Goodman, age 55, a whistleblowing accountant, and tossed him off a bridge. Simple as that. That's my kind of contract. No guns, no blood, just a oopsie-daisy and a hundred-foot drop. The body washed up two miles downstream where a few early morning fishermen found him.

Now here I am in a dark hallway, so dark in fact that I can't see two feet in front of me. Plenty of time has passed for my eyes to adjust but it's no help. I hesitate to use the mini flashlight attached to my right shoulder. I'm expecting a pack of rabid dogs ahead and I don't want any chance of alerting them to my presence. And when I say a pack of rabid dogs, I really just mean a group of four or five assholes that I'll likely have to put down on my way to the real target.

My pre-analysis for this mission left me no choice but to enter the building through a side door where the lock is faulty. Any other option would leave me with no element of surprise, and ultimately, I'd end up with guns blazing, blood flying, and failure in the mission. From my experiences on the Kill Team and in life, having an unsuspecting target is the single most important thing one can achieve. Even a few milliseconds worth of time advantage is often the difference in avoiding catastrophe.

I take small steps, using my memory of the layout to guide me. Emily provided me with a blueprint from the county clerk's office. Assuming there haven't been any heavy unpermitted remodels, I should be good. Eighteen half-strides and I come to a T. To the right another hallway with an open doorway at the end and the first source of light beyond that. My black tactical outfit should keep me hidden until I step through the threshold.

I'm ten feet from the opening to the room, leaning tight against the north wall. I have a custom twenty-round .45 millimeter drawn. The six-inch silencer on the end will muffle the noise by about eighty-five percent. That will help get me from point A to point B in this building without alerting the cavalry. There could be as many as ten people in here somewhere, by my best estimate. In the room before me, I can see only one.

The roughly forty-foot by forty-foot space is dimly lit, soft yellow. The one window is painted over black. There are two other doors, both on the opposite wall to where I am. There is a six-seater poker table right in the center with six chairs. To my left, there's a push cart against the wall with various bottles of alcohol, a bucket of ice, and several stacks of shot glasses and tumblers. The right wall has a wide TV stand with a Blu-ray player, a sound bar, and a fifty or sixty-inch flat screen TV on the top.

The only man in the room is standing at the poker table with his back to me, counting and dishing out stacks of poker chips. After placing a stack at one seating position, he takes a sip of his beverage. Poker night.

I basically have two choices: I can sneak up on the guy and try to get him unconscious before he sees me or I can kill him. The second one is easy and eliminates him from being a problem on the way out should he wake up. I don't care much for that option. One thing I told myself when I decided to join the organization was that I would work hard to avoid taking unnecessary lives. I find it highly unsavory. We are encouraged to support my preferred method, but I get the impression that some within the organization don't really give a shit either way. Like Amatto once told me, I'm part of the next generation that can set new standards and help move things in a specific direction. I plan to do just that.

Either way, I must move fast. Best way I can see to surprise him is rush in and hit him, then move even faster to my target.

I charge forward and I'm on top of him before he can even register the fact he's heard footsteps. As he turns to his right to face me, I smash him right in the side of the head with the butt of my gun. He crashes on top of the poker table, scattering chips on the surface and onto the floor. He's out cold. I wipe the blood from my gun on his pants leg. He's going to have one hell of a bump from that blow.

I hear a voice. A laugh. Another voice. They're getting closer. Shit!

Out of the corner of my eye I see a light come on in the hallway I entered by. I hear two more voices from that direction. Double shit!

I'm about to be surrounded. I turn slightly to my left so I can see both doors. I keep the gun at my side and put my other hand on the gun at my left waist. This is about to get nasty.

To my right, three guys come into the room and are suddenly not laughing, not so chatty. To my left, two more enter. When they all see their man on the table, all five draw a weapon and there's a quick succession of hammer clicks. I begin to plan my next moves.

I take a few subtle steps back. I hide my weapon behind me. I've been working with Vick on my close-range, multiple target, handgun accuracy, as it's not one of my strong suits. I've improved, thankfully. Testing, testing ... bang, bang, bang.

In a matter of seconds, I've analyzed my enemies. I have one path forward and one path back. These guys are not going to let me out of here alive, that's a fact. They can see the tactical gear I'm wearing. I'm clearly not here to sell Mary Kay. Mercurio's been in the game awhile, so I have to assume all these guys are capable, strong, and will act without hesitation, regardless of my size and gender.

The guy front and center on the right is standing bold and confident. There's your leader. Need to bust him down first. He'll be the best shot and will command the others into action, so if he goes down, chaos should ensue.

"I don't suppose I can convince you guys to just let me out of here? I was looking for that new bagel place and accidently stumbled in here."

"Do we look stupid to you?" the leader says. "You know what, don't answer that. We know what you're here for."

"So, what is it, the outfit? The outfit gives it away, right?

"That gigantic fuckin' piece you hiding behind your back too."

I bring my gun forward, slowly and look at it. "This thing? Found it in the street. Don't even know how to use it."

"Bullshit. That's a custom job. I've never even seen a gun like that. And what's that? A six or eight-inch silencer?"

"Six. Won't fit in my favorite holster with the eight."

"Let's cut the crap woman. Put the cannon down. Right now."

"I can't do that."

"I guarantee you this ain't gonna end well for you. In case you can't count, there are five of us and only one of you.

You're gonna end up with thirty bullet holes by the time you squeeze off two rounds. Not great odds."

I nod a few times. "That makes sense. You do kind of have me in a pickle here." I'm tiring of the chit-chat and ready to get down to business. I take two deep breaths and go to work.

As quick as I can, I snatch the leg of the poker table closest to me and pull it hard upwards while dragging back a few feet. Their unconscious friend falls hard to the floor, poker chips scattering everywhere, his glass of vodka sliding off and shattering on the floor. Before I can duck down, two bullets whiz by to my right. I crouch and fire off six shots from around the right side of the table.

The guy to my far right takes a shot to his left cheek and drops. The leader takes a hit to the left shoulder and his right bicep. He manages to stay on his feet. The other three bullets hit the wall behind them.

I crouch as low as I can. Bullets are flying everywhere. Splinters from the table spray into the air all around me. I'm losing my barricade faster than I had hoped.

I decide to make a bold move. I roll to the left, hop to my feet, and charge toward the two guys on the left with my weapon firing out in front of me. I skitter one step to the right and then back left to avoid getting hit. They both suffer fatal wounds to their heads and torsos. A trail of bullet holes follows me out of the door.

I fall into the corner to the left, just past the doorway.

"Go get that bitch!" the leader shouts. Footsteps ensue.

I peek out and fire three bullets into the approaching man's upper body. He staggers and drops just short of the two bodies near the doorway.

I notice the leader has retreated to the hallway from which he entered. He has two pretty harsh wounds that won't necessarily kill him, so long as he gets medical attention soon. Otherwise, he may bleed out. The trail of blood on the floor demonstrates that perfectly and will lead me right to him.

I decide I can't take any chances, so I fire off two quick

shots into the chest of the unconscious guy I had originally left alive and cautiously head down the hallway. There are two doors to choose from: one at the far end and one in the middle of the wall to my right. The blood smear on the floor guides me.

I walk the six feet to the first door, careful not to slip on the mess. I give two hard knocks on the green wooden door.

"Ohhhh, Mercurio! I know you're in there!"

I grab the doorknob and just as I start to turn it, I hear a loud crash and glass breaking, like someone tossed a chair through a window.

I rush in to find exactly that. The man I trailed in is slumped over in a rust-orange leather lounge chair to the right, lifeless. To my left, the broken window. Fuck! Mercurio has left the fucking building. Not good. Not good.

I put a finger to the earpiece in my ear and hold it there on the tiny button.

"Betamax, this is VHS, target is on the move. I repeat, target jumped out a fuckin' window on the south end of the building."

"Shit. You need an intercept?" Vick replies.

I run to the window and look out. Mercurio is limping his way through the tiny parking lot toward an overgrown pasture.

"Head to the far end of the field south of the building. I'm after him. If he makes it to the other side, take him."

"Copy that."

I climb out of the window and almost sprain my ankle trying to plant my feet amongst the debris on the ground. I stumble out of the mess and run full speed at Mercurio. He's struggling to get through the brush. Must have injured himself in the same way I almost did.

I'm within about twenty feet of him now, so I slow down and take careful aim.

"It's over, man."

He stops in his tracks, breathing heavy, leaning over a bit.

"I didn't have a choice. They pinched me, hard. I got kids,

a wife."

"I don't care."

"I was getting out after all this, leavin' it behind. Gonna move my family away. You gotta family?"

I'm walking toward Mercurio, cautious and slow. I need to assume he has a gun.

"Still don't care." I'm fifteen feet from him. I have my gun pointed right at the base of his neck. I catch sight of Vick about two hundred feet away. He has a sniper rifle on a tripod, his left eye in the scope.

"Not an ounce of humanity in ya? I never really hurt anyone. Just trying to make a living. You wanna take a father from his kids?"

"It's not my decision. I'm just doing my job. People don't like rats."

I keep a stern demeanor, a robotic tone in my voice, but his words annoyingly resonant with me. My family disappeared without a trace about twenty years ago, a topic I'm currently looking into. The only information I've ever had about their disappearance came from the children's home I grew up in. I've never questioned the story they told me, so when Ollie laid that bomb on me at the Academy, my head has been spinning ever since. What else don't I know? I'm starting to question everything I've ever believed, and in a world of secrets and lies and killing, I'm becoming generally uneasy and paranoid. That's a dangerous state of mind to be in.

"Well, if I'm going to die, so are you." He starts a slow turn toward me.

In my earpiece from Vick, "Grenade! Get down!"

I flip around, diving down and away from Mercurio. On my way to the ground, I hear the bang and feel the percussion. As I hit dirt and brush, I cover my head, dust and smoke billowing outward from where Mercurio once stood. All manner of soil and plant material scatters, not to mention the now detached parts of Mercurio.

I roll to my side and lift my head. There is only smoke

where the man once stood. My ear without the earpiece is ringing. What little sound there is has a tunnel effect. I get to my feet and brush myself off using my free hand.

"VHS, you okay?"

"I'm fine. Can't say the same for your boy here." I reach the body. There are pieces of him scattered about, some bigger than others. I just about lose my lunch. I've seen blood. I've seen dead bodies. They don't really bother me. But this. Phew. It's pretty gnarly.

"I'm heading back to the van," Vick says. "Get out of there. We'll just leave him be. It'll look like a suicide."

"It *was* a suicide. We didn't touch him. That explosion is going to draw attention though, so we need to scoot. I'll be at the rendezvous point in less than five minutes."

"Be safe ... and hurry."

"Copy that."

We have a five-hour drive from Elmira to NYC. That's five hours of contemplating the mission, hearing Vick ask me for the hundredth time if I'm okay, me sitting in deep thought and staring out of the window, looking beyond the scenery, the buildings, the traffic, and ultimately, right into the face of my past.

The note Ollie passed me at headquarters said: Want to know who you really are? Then he whispered the words Allister Cole to me. Then he walked away. That was months ago now. I've had no time to even think much about it, let alone pursue it, but Mercurio's words have me itching again. Some mysteries are better left unsolved, or so I've heard. That might be true. In my case, I didn't realize a mystery even existed. Now that I know there is one, and it revolves around my parents, their disappearance, and who I may or may not be, there's no way in hell I can let that one go. And I'm no dummy. Clearly, because of the covert way in which Ollie chose to share this news with me, the organization cannot know about my efforts to solve this mystery. It does raise the bigger question of why.

For now, I'll bide my time, and when I can, I'll start poking around until I find whatever truth might be out there for me. My past is already a complicated one, and I'm certain this will only make it worse.

All these thoughts of my history have forced me to remember a great many things, difficult things. Being in that rundown former strip club surrounded by five guys out to do me harm sure took me back. It wasn't the first time, and I'm certain it won't be the last.

2

Five Years Ago

It was a Friday, past midnight. The mid-August air was suffocating, the kind of high humidity heat that if a person had to spend too much time outdoors they'd need to roll their underwear off at the end of the day. Yeah. It was gross.

By that time, I had been on my own and living a street life for the better part of five years. For anyone, that type of minute to minute existence could unravel the best of us, but for a woman of short stature and subjectively good looks, it was too often a nightmarish life of learning to fight, learning to cope, learning to live in the shadows just to avoid any unnecessary attention.

I was twenty years old then and shacked up in the basement of an elderly Japanese gentleman that caught me stealing vegetables from his garden. He didn't threaten me, didn't call the police. Instead, he consoled me, asked me if I was okay. I actually broke character and cried a little while I shared some of my life story with him. About how my parents disappeared without a trace when I was five years old. How I spent the better part of my childhood in a children's home mixed with a few scattered weeks of foster family life. I don't think I had ever spilled so much about my life to anyone, ever. There was a curiously instantaneous trust, like

11

I'd known him my whole life and had often gone to him when I just needed someone to listen.

He fed me, made me try warm sake, and let me shower. In fact, I had a few too many sakes that night and started calling him Mr. Sake, a name he embraced for the evening, though his real name happened to be Ichiro Tomita. People close to him called him Tom. When he offered me up his basement as a temporary living space, I respectfully declined, but he insisted.

The space was about as inviting as a crypt but it gave me a safe place to lay my head at night. It wasn't a truly finished basement either. It was dank and dimly lit. The walls were cheap wood paneling that had been glued directly to the concrete block. The floor was also concrete save for the eight-foot by ten-foot beige rug centered on the space. In the corner was a cheaply assembled shower stall, a toilet, and a pedestal sink, rather filthy and with no real privacy. As bad as this might seem, I've actually had worse. Imagine that.

Tom helped me get a real job as a prep cook at a local restaurant, one within walking distance of the house, and one of only three legit jobs I've ever had. I had no real desire to be an upstanding citizen but there was something about the way Tom proposed the idea that made it hard not to at least try. In any case, I decided to reciprocate his kindness and go for it.

After working there for about six weeks chopping and cleaning all the vegetables, making sure the cook's line had all the food and plate prepping accoutrements, and doing whatever menial tasks the real cooks demanded, I overheard some of the backend staff discussing a woman they knew that walked home alone from work every night. As the details emerged, it became obvious they were talking about me. I was standing outside the breakroom filling pans with tomatoes, onions, and parsley, so they had no idea I overheard them. As they rose from their chairs, I scrambled away.

I didn't know if their words were anything more than

locker room banter amongst boys or a real discussion about following me home, attacking me, and ultimately, raping me. I didn't really know them but I had always assumed well-functioning adults don't openly discuss that type of behavior, although, in the cruel world I live in, nothing like that would have been surprising. For whatever reason, I didn't take it seriously.

Fast forward a week and that conversation had all but left my mind. To that point, my paranoid defense mechanisms were only blossoming, more a self-developed, fear-based skill with no real focus. After that night, I honed those skills as a watcher, a listener. I would become acutely aware of how many people were in a room, the sound of approaching bodies, the unsheathing of a knife.

Once again, like every Friday night after a dinner shift that ended with the lesser of us kitchen employees cleaning up the mess created by a chaotic rush, I left Solara's Grill alone, on my way home and looking forward to a shower to help get the smell of restaurant off me.

Like anytime I'm alone on the street at night, I kept my eyes and ears alert. I walked swiftly down the sidewalk. I wouldn't call the neighborhood bad but it wasn't good either. There were rundown houses scattered amongst old brick buildings. Some were taverns, others an old record store, a tattoo parlor, a t-shirt screen print shop. During the daytime, there was little reason for people to fear being down there, but at night, when the only businesses open were the bars and what few houses there were tended to be abandoned, best to get where you're going as quickly as possible without drawing any attention.

With each step and each drip of sweat from my brow, I longed for the cool temps of my basement room. There was no air conditioning down there, but in the summer, it was easily fifteen degrees cooler than whatever the temperature was outside. I just wanted to kick up my feet with a cold beer before falling asleep. Work was stupid busy, and no amount of chopping and dicing and cleaning seemed enough. I thought seriously at one point of using the mandolin to take off the tip of one my fingers just so I could go chill in the emergency room for a few hours. And by chill, I mean sit in the air conditioning. I figured, hey, I'll have nine fingers left and what do we really use our pinkies for anyway.

It was when I hit the third of my ten-block walk home that I heard the chatter. From an unknown distance behind me, the voices of a group of men cut through the humid night air. I was already walking fast yet they had managed to gain. I peeked over my shoulder and saw a group of four men but could not make out who they were. My pace quickened. My heart sank. I swallowed hard with nervous energy.

I came to the front entrance of a place called Slappy's Tavern and decided to stop. I could see lights on inside but had no idea if they were still open.

The group got closer, laughing and talking as they walked.

I got edgy and started planning the way I might make a quick escape or talk my way out of a bad situation.

I leaned back against the wall to the left of the bar's front door.

The men were twenty feet away, then fifteen, then ten, then past me without a look. I did my best version of disinterested and I guess it worked. I thought for sure they were some of the guys from Solara's Grill, guys I had never even bothered to learn the names of as I had no interest in knowing them beyond dishwasher number one, anonymous busboy, or lame-ass fry cook.

I stayed put until the men were out of sight. Already spent from a long evening at the restaurant, I started again on my way home, this time pushing myself to a light jog.

I got about forty strides down the sidewalk when a blockade emerged from between two buildings. There were five of them. Three of them were the guys from the work, the other two I had never seen before. A cloud had emerged with them, like someone filled a barrel with weed and french fries and beer, set it on fire, and rolled it down the street.

I stopped dead in my tracks. I took a step toward the

street but was quickly encircled. I had no weapons on me, no pepper spray, and not so much as a set of fingernail clippers. The knapsack on my back had a copy of *The Girl with the Dragon Tattoo*, a half-empty bottle of water, a few panty liners, my keys (because I didn't like carrying them in my pocket), and a baggie of dehydrated apple chips given to me by Tom. Even MacGyver would have had a hard time assembling that random bunch of shit into anything useful.

"You look lost," the fry cook said.

"I'm just trying to get home. Please let me pass."

"It's dangerous out here. Lotta whackos running 'round," the dishwasher said.

"Like you?" I said.

One of the guys I'm not familiar with slapped the dishwasher in the shoulder and laughed. "She told yo ass."

"Shut the fuck up, DiMarco," the dishwasher responded.

"Maybe you need an escort," the fry cook said.

"I don't. You know we work together, right?"

"Yeah. We've had our eyes on you. You look like you like to party."

I made a move to pass them but was denied. I tried again with the same result. I could feel them starting to close in on me, the conversation boring them.

"I'm tired. I live just up the street. Let me pass."

The busboy took a final swig of his beer bottle and tossed it fifty feet down the street. I hoped the noise of shattering glass might alert someone. No such luck.

I had been on my own for a while at that point, so I knew how to handle myself, but the five-on-one odds were not in my favor. If I had had any kind of blunt object, maybe. I'd long been thinking about carrying a stun gun, a potential size equalizer, but had yet to pull the trigger on buying one. That encounter pushed it to the top of my to-do list.

"Grab her," the dishwasher commanded.

The busboy and DiMarco seized my arms. I writhed but it was of no use. I was overpowered. The fry cook stepped forward, brandishing a six-inch blade.

"Please don't do this. Come on guys." I could feel my words falling on deaf ears. I screamed for help.

With his free hand, the fry cook slapped me straight across the face. "Quiet down, you stupid bitch. There's no one out here to help you." Careful not to cut me, he took the tip of his blade and slit my t-shirt open from just below my breasts and all the way through the collar, revealing my black sports bra. "That's not very sexy. Then again, you really ain't got much to work with, do ya?"

I had been scared before that moment but anger quickly became my driving force.

"Take her down there," the fry cook said as he pointed to a dark area between the two buildings they had emerged from.

I dragged my feet and twisted myself free from the busboy. I seized the opportunity to cold-cock DiMarco dead center to his face with all the power I could muster. I could feel the cartilage crushing beneath my knuckles and blood sprayed from his nose. He released his grip on my arm and buckled.

Free from their grasp, I bolted toward the street. I figured I'd have a slight advantage in a full out run considering they'd been smoking pot and drinking. I underestimated them.

The fry cook jumped into the street and cut me off, the busboy right behind him. DiMarco was on his knees whining and trying in vain to get his nose to stop bleeding. The dishwasher was at his side trying to help. The fifth guy hadn't said or done anything. Not sure if he was just too high to be involved or just didn't care to be.

I tried to bowl through the two-man blockade but failed. The fry cook grabbed me by the arms, the knife still in his right hand, and wrestled me hard to the ground. I hit the asphalt with the weight of us both, directly onto my right shoulder. I felt a pop and a sharp pain.

"Ahhh!" I screamed.

"Jesus," the busboy said. "Sounds like you broke something."

The fry cook released his grip on me. When he noticed the knife had pierced my skin just beneath the shoulder blade, he nonchalantly plucked it out and got back on his feet, leaving me writhing on the ground.

I attempted to get up but the fire in my shoulder wouldn't allow it. Instead, I used my good arm to drag myself back to the curb. When I reached the concrete, I was barely conscious. I thought I heard a familiar voice. There was shouting, a lot of commotion, thuds and smacking sounds and grunts.

I struggled to keep my eyes open as the pain had become nearly unbearable. With my head resting on the curb, a man approached. He knelt at my side and revealed his face. Tom.

I had never been so happy to see someone in my entire life.

"Thank you," I whispered.

"You're bleeding. Are you hurt anywhere else?"

"That same shoulder popped out or broke."

"Can you sit up?"

Tom grabbed my uninjured arm and helped me get my butt on the curb. My right arm hung loose at my side.

As gently as he could, Tom inspected the area near my collarbone and socket.

I hollered when he grazed the uppermost part of my arm.

"Sorry, kiddo. Your arm is out of the socket and you may have broken your collarbone. The cut is not too deep but will probably need a few stitches."

"Oh shit. I can't afford to go to the hospital. What am I gonna do?"

"You don't have much choice here. I can put your arm back in but you'll need a doctor for that cut and if anything is broken." He took my right hand and elevated it. He lined it up using his left hand as a guide. "Brace yourself. This is not going to be pleasant."

I closed my eyes and gnashed my teeth.

My mouth went to scream but I blacked out.

I opened my eyes and found Tom sitting in a chair next to me. I managed to smile despite my morphine clouded mind. I recognized the space as Tom's living room.

"Just rest easy," Tom said.

"What happened?"

"I took you to a doctor friend of mine. Got you an x-ray. Luckily, your collarbone was not broken. Arm was out of the socket and your shoulder is severely sprained. The knife wound may have caused some minor nerve damage but you're all stitched up."

"Shit. How am I going to pay for that? Hospitals are expensive."

"It wasn't exactly a hospital, not one for humans anyway."

"What?"

"Dr. Allerton is a veterinarian. I took you to an animal hospital. He's a very good friend."

"How long am I going to be like this? I can't afford to miss work." As I mentioned work, it reminded me of the encounter that put me in this situation. "What happened on the street last night?"

"It became abundantly clear that you need to work on your self-defense skills. Someone like you cannot afford to be passive about protecting yourself. You live in dark places with dark people."

"Someone like me?"

"Not to offend ... but you are a woman, a small woman. You're nice to people. They'll take advantage."

"I'm not that nice."

"Look, I know you've been on your own for years and you've figured out to survive out here, but one day, when you put your guard down for two seconds, you're going to fall ... hard. Like you almost did last night. Imagine if I had not shown up."

"But you did, and I'm grateful for that. And on that point, can you clarify something for me?"

"I'll try."

"How the hell did you handle those guys all by yourself?

Jesus, you're like eighty years old."

"I'm not that old, smartass. But I used to be like you. I'm a small Japanese man living in a bad neighborhood. At some point, in order to survive down here, I needed to learn to defend myself. You know that restaurant you work at?"

"Yeah. What about it?"

"That used to be mine. I owned it for almost thirty-five years. It was a sushi place back then. Authentic Japanese cuisine."

"You owned that? Wow."

"I did. But early on, we got robbed several times a month, including one particularly bad incident where my wife and I ended up on the floor with shotguns at our heads."

"No shit?"

"No shit. And of course, the police were no help. They didn't even want to come down here. It was much worse back then, like a condensed version of New Jack City. I decided to take matters into my own hands. I learned to use a gun and hid one on the premises. But that was for extreme situations only, so I took what I had lying around. I started taking Tae Kwan Do at the Y, and every morning before we opened, I spent thirty minutes in the back alley with a broom handle teaching myself how to use it like a Bo Staff. Eventually, the criminals stayed away when they realized I could handle myself."

"That's incredible. I want you to teach me."

"Once you're all healed up, we can talk about it again."

"Good. Thank you. Thank you for everything."

3

The keystrokes fall like a storm surge on pavement, the black screen of the laptop filling quickly with code very few people on the Earth can understand. The pace at which the hacker works is based purely on their desire to stay undetected. Like a round of fencing, the moves and countermoves are lightning quick: parry, cut, block, thrust, feint, parry, thrust.

Access to the private and heavily guarded network is the goal. Once inside, only the simplest of information will be easily attainable, the more secretive intel buried deep behind redundant firewalls, system access alerts, global signal redistribution, and multi-key encryption. The hacker understands that there is almost no possibility of beating all of these defenses, so the best way in is through someone else's access. Getting that will be the hard part. Screen and keystroke mirroring would be a good start, but even that would require local access, either directly through a terminal within the network or a piece of malware planted through an email account associated with the network.

Email plants have been sent. Now the hacker must wait for an unsuspecting target to open an attachment or click a link from within one of the emails. The people working for the company, however, aren't stupid. They've all been well-trained when it comes to technological security, but humans make mistakes, even the smartest ones, and the hacker is counting on that. It's really just a waiting game.

4

We arrive at the Kill Team house in upstate New York just after dark. Both Vick and I are exhausted. Along the way, I made him detour about forty-five minutes for a strawberry milkshake. He wasn't pleased, but considering I'm Point on this mission, I'm in charge until we get back safely, so he has to do as I say. I don't remember him complaining when that luscious strawberry hit his lips. "See," I said. "See. Instant mood enhancer and body relaxer." He shrugged me off, but as he sucked on that straw, his deep sighs told the story.

The first gate surrounding the forty-acre property is a total smoke screen. There's a simple white farm fence along the front with a short but heavy steel gate painted red. We have to get out of the car to manually open and close the damn thing. It's secured with a simple pad lock. The key is under a rock at the base of the hinge post. This gate and fence are not stopping anyone.

Once past the initial gate, about a quarter of a mile down the gravel drive, we come to a heavily tree-lined area. Behind those trees is a well-camouflaged sixteen-foot tall fence with barbed wire that only opens when someone carrying a special fob comes close. That fob is also what allows us access into the building at headquarters, a very recent upgrade to the facility, and it can be programmed to allow or deny entry into every single room of the building. For example, Madame K's office door will only open with her fob or her secretary's. This extra measure of security within that place has me thinking something is up. For years and up until about six months ago, they never felt the need for such stringent door security, especially considering how difficult, if not impossible, it is for people to get in the building in the first place. That kind of door-to-door paranoia gives me the impression that all is not well within the ranks of the company I work for – Advanced Weapons Tech. Something to keep an eye on.

Past the green barricade, the drive winds around to the right for another quarter of a mile until we reach the house. On the outside, it's a crusty old white farmhouse, and I remember the first time I saw it, I was like, "What kind of shithole are they putting us up in? Are they joking?"

My disdain turned to awe as we walked through the front door that first time. The interior spoke more of modern royalty - a palace of white and gray, streaky Italian marble floors, crisp, clean lines, state of the art everything right down to the lighting controlled by phone app. The parlor to the right is set up as a simple sitting area with a navy-blue leather sofa and matching chairs. The left bares a grand curved staircase to the second floor where there are three bedrooms and three baths, all three master suites, really.

A hallway leading to the back of the house has two doors, one a half bath, the other a staircase to the basement which serves as a mini operations center. The door to that is, of course, fob granted access only, so even if someone manages to get on the property and into the house, they'll have one hell of a time getting down there.

The back of the house is a large kitchen and dining area complete with an island and a spacious pantry for food and weapons storage. Yes, I said weapons storage. There's a clever little panel that when activated reveals a hidden cache of arms, should we be invaded by the Russians or something. This is a separate stash of weapons from the main one's downstairs and in the shed near the shooting range. There's a door off the dining room too that houses our small exercise room.

We head straight back to the kitchen area to greet Emily. She has her eyes and fingers in her laptop. Her face speaks of deep concentration, and to be honest, it makes me a little nervous.

"Everything okay?" I ask.

"Hi guys, ummm," Emily says without breaking stride. "Give me one second."

"We'll just go get cleaned up and come back down and talk in a bit," Vick says.

Emily gives us a couple of quick nods and just keeps going with whatever she's doing.

Vick and I look to each other and he shrugs. We head upstairs to shower and change. I have a bottle of scotch in my room I'm desperately looking forward to pouring a glass from. A strawberry milkshake has only a limited span of stress relieving ability. Now that we're back home, it's time for the real deal.

Mercurio was our third CLAK (Contract Level Alpha Kill) assignment since graduating from the Kill Academy nine months ago. My resistance to the actual killing part has lightened up, although, the job still gets to my nerves in an unsettling way that I can't quite explain. Perhaps it's just the idea that with each contract we execute, my own life is at significant risk, whether it's from being killed or being caught. I don't think I'll ever get used to riding that razor's edge.

Living at the house with Vick and Emily has been pretty good. It's infinitely better than being at the academy. Even though I know we are being watched because there are multiple cameras outside and one in every room of the house, save for the bedrooms and baths, and thankfully no audio at all, there's a sense of freedom here. We workout when we want, we practice weapons proficiency when we want, we watch TV when we want. Unfortunately, we can't leave the property unless we're on a mission. Our faces cannot be seen locally. Hell, even our groceries are brought to us by company people. Granted, we can order anything we want, but a frozen pizza is just not the same as a bubbling hot Giordano's.

That's Evie's favorite and mine too. I think about the Leer family every day, wishing I could see them or at least call. In the nine months since I saved Evie from the grip of that asshole Terrance, I wonder how they're doing, how much Evie has grown and if she's still wearing those damn shoes, and if they're holding their own financially. Direct contact with them, especially after that suspicious training mission that took me back to Baltimore and put them in danger, is not an option, not right now anyway. At my first and best opportunity, I do plan to check in on them, maybe sneak them some money. It'll have to be done covertly and at a safe distance. I wouldn't dare put them at risk again.

With a towel around my torso and my hair in a damp ponytail, I sit on the edge of my bed and sip on the glass of scotch I poured before I went to the bathroom to clean up.

I'm trying hard not to think about Mercurio and the final state he was left in. Hard to scrub that image away. Overall, the mission went well. I would rather he have been alone so there wouldn't have been so much collateral damage, but we knew going in that wasn't going to happen. When a guy like Mercurio finds out there's a price on his head, he'll surround himself with as many lackeys as he thinks necessary to ensure his safety. Too bad for him, I've been well-trained in the murdering chaotic arts. Too bad for his comrades as well.

I planted a gun on Mercurio similar to my own and then set the building on fire. When the locals investigate the scene, hopefully they'll believe he killed all the people inside, set it on fire in an attempt to cover it up, then went out in the field and blew himself up because he just couldn't deal with the guilt, or maybe just because he knew he was fucked. At the very least, the people of that county will have an interesting story to tell about a criminal entrepreneur, a torched rundown strip club, and a mass murder that is just too weird to understand.

Eventually, Vick, Emily and I end up at the dining room table together for a casual team debriefing. We do this after each contract. We are also required to visit HQ for a more official one.

"So, what had your attention so fiercely when we got home?" I ask Emily. "You had some serious concentration-face."

"Yeah, we need to discuss that," Emily says. "I've been picking up some usual but very discreet traffic on our network. Still trying to figure out what the hell it is." Emily is normally soft spoken, even-keeled, coy, but there is a measure of urgency in her voice I've not heard.

"Like, on our house network or the company network?" Vick asks.

"Best as I can tell, just ours, but it's still unclear. It's really strange, like someone is knocking on the door but not really trying to get in. Like they're just trying the locks, maybe looking for vulnerabilities."

"Maybe corporate is testing you," I say.

"I thought about that, and maybe that's it, but I'm concerned. Whomever is doing this, it's not random. Our specific network is being targeted."

"Meaning ... they know who we are?" Vick asks.

"Possibly. That's why I'm so worried. I'll keep tracking it and if anything coalesces, I'll let you guys know. Just keep your ears and eyes open. Should you notice anything weird around here or when you're on missions, tell me right away, no matter how small."

"Ten-four," Vick says with double thumbs up.

"How'd the mission go?"

"Kind of wild, actually," I say. "Didn't even have to take him out in the end. He killed himself with a fuckin' grenade, if you can believe that. Almost got me too. Vick saw it in time, thankfully."

"What? A grenade?" Emily's face is begging for an explanation.

"Yeah. After I had him backed into a room, he tossed a

chair through a window and jumped out, then tried to run away into a field. I chased him and told Vick to cut him off on the other side. When he stopped, he begged me to let him go, gave me that whole 'I got a family' bullshit. Then he blew himself up, hoping to take me out too. Vick saw the grenade and warned me. Thank you again, Vick."

"Of course," Vick responds. "We're a team. We have to look out for each other."

"It comes easy to you," I say. "You're ex-military. You're trained that way. We're still getting used to that, as I'm sure Emily would agree. With our background, being on our own and never trusting anyone is key to survival."

Emily nods in agreement. "I rarely had anyone I could count on. I like it here though. Nice feeling to know you guys have my back."

"All of our lives depend on it," Vick says. "Just keep that in mind. Our success directly correlates to our working as a team and trusting one another completely. This work is too dangerous for us to expect anything else."

"So, when we go to HQ for the official debriefing, should I mention the possible hack? Perhaps we should just keep it to ourselves for now, at least until I know more."

"What do you think, Vick? I say ... let's try and work the problem ourselves, for the time being."

Vick ponders the idea, rubs his chin stubble. "Yeah, let's just keep it here. But if at any point this thing becomes something tangible we can't deal with it, we tell Marty or Tisha, at the very least. Agreed?"

Emily and I both nod.

Vick rises from his chair. "I was gonna throw a burger on the grill to go with that potato salad we got left in the fridge. Either of you want me to throw one on for you?"

Like an ethereally connected set of twins, Emily and I raise our hands simultaneously and then giggle.

"Thanks, Vick. I'd like cheddar on mine," I say.

"Me too," Emily adds.

"Roger that," Vick says.

"Do you have to use walkie-talkie speak even when we're at home?" I chide him. He only does it because he knows it annoys me.

He's already walking away and gives me an over the shoulder upside down middle finger. "Copy that."

I shake my head.

Emily laughs. "You two are weird. My brother and I used to argue like that when we lived at home.

"I never had siblings, so I guess I'm just making up for it. Now that he's out of the room, though, I wanted to talk to you about that little thing I'm having you help with. How's it going?"

"Well, I was able to map out the full scope of the cameras and I've identified the blind spots, what few there are."

"Oh?"

"I won't be able to disable any cameras, not without sounding the alarms at AWT, but ... hang on, let me pull up the schematic." Emily turns back to her laptop, and with a few keystrokes and cursor movements, she flips it around to show me her screen. "The red dots are the cameras. Those three blue dotted lines represent paths that someone could walk and be out of the view of any camera."

I study the screen. This doesn't leave me many options. I see a narrow path away from the house leading to the edge of the property where the giant tree line and fence are. In the dark and dressed all in black, I think I can make it. After that, it will get more complicated.

I have a multi-faceted plan to escape the asylum, just to get a few moments completely to myself, and of course, do some research in the hunt for any clues to my past. When we graduated from the Kill Academy, Ollie left me with a name and a strong impression that something in my past is not what it seems. I have no idea, even to this day, what the hell it means. I just haven't had the time or privacy to look into it. With some luck, that is about to change. When we return from our debriefing at headquarters tomorrow, I will put my plan into motion.

5

The rain is coming down hard today. If it keeps up, my plan to leave the house tonight might have to get put on hold. There's no way I can walk for six miles in the dark, soaking wet, and not get pneumonia or something.

The three of us are in a completely and utterly conspicuous large black SUV with fully tinted windows on our way to headquarters to report on our latest mission. Should be uneventful for the most part. Having that little after mission chit-chat with Dina will be the only downer of the day. How do you feel? I feel great. I just killed five people for money and almost got blown up by psycho grenade guy. It'll take the crime scene people four hours to find all the bits and pieces of him. I'm fine, I'm fine, I'm fine.

We say almost nothing to one another on the long drive in, all of us instead choosing to have our eyes locked onto cell phone screens. Every minute I have to fight the temptation to do an internet search for Allister Cole. It will be one of the first things I do when I get free tonight and get my hands on a pre-paid phone.

The city of New York is bustling in a way that only NYC can. Aside from the traffic and the sheer number of people around, the noise is what catches my greatest attention. Compared to the stark, natural silence of the Kill Team house and its property, the city is almost deafening. And of course,

29

by natural silence, I don't mean true silence, but something more akin to the gentle hum of the Earth breathing. The trees creak in the wind, the insects banter, the birds flutter their wings and sing like no one, or maybe everyone, is listening. It's a chorus so subtle it can lull a person to sleep. Natural silence.

I've always been a city girl but that country life ain't no joke, and I'm sure as hell getting used to it. I do miss the bay and coffee shops and kittens. I don't miss the constantly looking over my shoulder and random people and wondering where the hell I'm going to lay my head each night. When the time comes, I'll no doubt have a difficult time deciding which I prefer as my permanent way of life. Decisions, decisions.

The driver drops us at the elevator and we ride down to the levels where we were once trained. They repainted the walls and changed the carpet since our last visit. Gray and burgundy and various shades thereof in place of the old gray, gray, and more gray, and just in case you had any humanity left, splashes of black.

I still find it weird that Ollie and Dina have offices down here and not up where Madame K is. I get the Dean and the other instructors having theirs down here, but Ollie is second in command and Dina is, well ... Dina. Seems cruel by some measure I can't calculate.

There's still no new class of trainees and probably won't be for some time. The organization currently employs two solo assassins and the one Kill Team, and that's all they need at the moment. I have no idea who the second assassin is, the one not named Amatto. Apparently, it's some deep cover thing. Amatto won't likely show his face around here much anymore either, which sucks. I feel like I had a real connection with him, even in our limited exposure.

We reach Ollie's office and the door is open. He's sitting at his desk, reading something on his laptop. He looks up when he sees us standing there.

"Come in, Vick. You two go get a drink and I'll send Vick for you in a bit."

Vick enters. Emily and I head to the cafeteria. It's customary for Ollie to interview us individually after each mission. We'll each have to meet with Dina right afterwards too. With two successful missions under our belts, I feel we're doing well enough not to trouble anyone.

I grab my usual coffee and a muffin. Emily snags a diet cola.

"You not gonna eat anything?" I realize I sound like what Gabby must to her siblings. Motherly.

"Too nervous. I might hurl. These briefings, I don't know. They make me tense."

"Ah," I dismiss. "Piece of cake. Everything went well."

"I know. I'm still worried about that thing. I need to figure it out before something bad happens."

"You'll get it. I'm not worried. Personally, I'm more worried about talking to Dina. She's like a cockroach crawling around in your ear trying to eat its way into your brain. I don't like being psycho-analyzed, in case you can't tell."

"That's a really disturbing image. Thank you for that."

I sip on my coffee. "That's why they keep me around. My own mind is way more fucked up than anything they could throw our way."

"You still a go for launch on that thing you're planning?"

"If the rain stops, yes. Otherwise, not yet."

"Do be careful," Emily lowers to a whisper. "If you get caught."

"I will. I just have a lot of questions that need to be answered and it's not safe for me to do it on company time and equipment, if you know what I'm saying."

Emily nods. "More than you know."

I sit down in the lone chair in front of Ollie's desk. His office is even smaller than Dina's, which is really starting to feel like a punishment. His desk is clean. He has an office phone, a laptop, a small stack of yellow mini legal pads, and a large coffee mug filled with his favorite mechanical pencils. This guy is a list-maker, a note-taker, a prepper. What that really means is that he has an attention to detail that allows him to see things that others don't. I always keep that in mind when I speak to him.

There are no decorations, save for one framed large art print of the Sunset in Venice by Monet. Still trying to figure that one out. Maybe it wasn't even his choice, but maybe it was. There might be more to Ollie than anyone knows.

I'm working on a second cup of coffee while we chat.

"So, what'd Vick say?" I ask.

"The mission got messy, the end anyway."

"Yeah."

"Do you have anything specific you want to discuss about the mission, overall?" he asks.

"Not particularly."

"Good. You have any trouble with ... research?" His eyes widen.

I think about his meaning. Clearly, he's not referring to the mission. I have to be careful about how I answer. No idea who might be listening around here.

"Still trying to figure out how to be discrete."

Ollie scratches the back of his head, then opens one of desk drawers and pulls out a cell phone. He slides it across the desk to me. He grabs a mechanical pencil from his cup and writes something on the top yellow pad before tearing off that piece of paper and sliding it over too.

I grab the paper and read: There's one number programmed in it. Anonymous, secure. Call it if you need to talk to me. Use the phone for research.

I crumple the paper and put in my right pants pocket. I leave the phone for the moment.

"There's been some developments, so get on it or the trail will run cold. Always be prepared on any mission, watch your back, cover your tracks." He puts his left index finger to his lips, then lowers it. He mouths the words: Tell no one.

I'm starting to catch Emily's stomach churning paranoia. "You know, on the average mission, what kind of danger level, one to ten, are we going to see?" I hope he catches my meaning.

He puts up both his hands with all his fingers separated and extended. "Treat them all like tens, but most for Kill Teams will be sixes or sevens."

"Okay. Thanks."

"Dina wants to see you now. You can go." Ollie turns his attention to the computer on his desk.

I grab the phone and place it in the pocket with the ball of paper. I get up and head out the door.

"Be careful out there," Ollie says without looking up from his laptop.

I give him a backwards wave and continue on.

I settle into a chair in front of Dina's desk. It's been less than a year since I first met her, yet she seems to have aged five. Not so much in looks, but definitely in demeanor and energy. Just by the look on her face, I get the impression her tolerance for bullshit has become clouded.

"Another successful mission I see," Dina says.

"Yeah, a real explosive one."

"I read the report. Any of that bother you? Kind of a close call."

"It was a little gruesome. It's amazing how messy an exploding body is. Lot of fluids, lot of pieces. Kind of shocking, but I'm okay."

"Any issues sleeping, spontaneous anxiety?"

"None whatsoever. I don't really like taking the pills you guys give us, but they do help me bring focus to the missions."

"I just don't want you to think of it as being weak or somehow inadequate to experience these things. In this line of work, it would be weird NOT to be on edge from time to time."

"Understood."

"Everything at the house okay?"

"The house is great. Better than the dorms here, that's for

damn sure. I will admit, I wish I could leave when we're not on a mission, but I'm trying to focus on the positives."

"And your housemates?"

"What about'em?"

"Relationships okay? I know being a team player isn't something you were used to before coming here."

"They're great. It's what I imagine living with siblings would be like."

"Argue a lot?"

"Oh, hell yeah. Cats and dogs sometimes."

"Nothing too serious I hope."

"No. More like differences in lifestyle choices and personalities. Vick is very organized, keeps his bed made, loads the dish machine, whereas I am lazy and sloppy and don't give a rip about that stuff. I drop my shoes in the hallway and leave shit laying around. Drives him mad."

"Just try to keep it civil. You don't want lingering negativity getting in your heads, not with your lives in each other's hands."

"Roger that." I bust out laughing. "Now he's got me doing it. Fucker."

"What's so funny?"

"Nothing. Just one of those sibling things between Vick and myself."

"You're free to go then. Congratulations on your continued success."

"Thank you."

I go to the exercise room after leaving Dina just to see if anything has changed. Nothing has. The equipment is the same, the smell is the same, my overall disgust of hamster wheel type exercise is the same. I'm reminded of Marcus, Caleb, and Arnoux. I wonder whatever happened to them.

I imagine the Dean standing here giving us looks of disappointment at our progress. Feels like forever ago yet it hasn't even been a year.

"I knew you would miss me," the Dean says.

I just about fall over in surprise. As I twist around, I find her standing about three feet from me.

"Damn it, woman! You're gonna make me piss myself."

"Apparently, you need more training. Can't let people sneak up on you like that."

"I assumed this was a safe place."

"No place is ever safe. No place."

I acknowledge with a nod and we exchange a smile. "You're right. I have actually missed you. I won't touch a treadmill without your prodding."

"I can tell," the Dean says as she pinches the side of her abdomen mockingly.

"Hey! You're so mean."

"Keeps me alive ... and young."

"Whatever you say, but the ice cream keeps telling me everything will be okay."

"Care to join me for a run then?" The Dean hops on a treadmill and starts it up.

"Only because if I don't, you'll give me that disappointed scowl you're so famous for." I get on the treadmill next to her and start at a brisk walking pace.

The Dean takes a remote control from the treadmill console and turns on the TV, sets it to a streaming radio station playing 80s hard rock, and increases the volume just loud enough that we can still hear each other speak but no one else could.

"You like this work?" the Dean asks.

I hesitate to answer, feeling like the question is one that Dina would ask. The Dean, however, has always been square with me, so I have no reason not to be honest.

"Not particularly."

"Good. If you ever get comfortable with all this, then I'd be worried."

"I've never exactly been Mother Theresa."

"Mother Theresa was never really Mother Theresa. Good and evil, right and wrong, these are just constructs, ideals we use to justify our behavior."

"I don't really know what that means. It feels pretty fuckin' evil doing what we do around here. I've just accepted the fact that there are varying degrees."

"One person's evil is another's salvation."

"Is there a point to this philosophical exercise?" I bump up the speed on my treadmill to two miles per hour, with the distinct impression I'm running away from something and need to move faster.

"You're keener than many that have come through here. Certainly, you've felt the tremors of change, heard the whispers, perhaps you've even participated in that whispering."

"Maybe. What do you know about it? And what the hell does all this have to do with good and evil?"

"There's going to come a time soon when you'll have to choose between one version of what is right and another version that is a reflection of what is right, one that when you look in the mirror, only you will be able to see the truth of it."

I place my hands on the support bars and give her a queer stare. "You're one cryptic woman, you know that?" I don't let her answer. "So, what should I do when faced with this choice?"

"It's not a matter of what you should do, it's matter of what you will do. You'll redefine yourself in the name of vengeance and possibly end up dead because of it."

I hop off the belt with my feet to the side rails and shut off the treadmill. "That sounds bleak and you're starting to scare me."

The Dean keeps on running but looks me dead in the eyes. "It is ... and you should be." She turns her head back to the forward position, a clear end to the lesson.

"We're going to be leaving soon, so ... I guess I'll see you next time. It's been fun hearing another Li Xia enigma, as always." I step back off the treadmill and go to leave the exercise room.

The loud music suddenly stops. "Josey."

I stop at the door and turn around. The Dean's face is one I've never seen – somber and filled with worry. "Do be careful."

"I will," I say with confidence, but the bravado is a lie. I'm scared shitless. I turn and leave. As I walk over to the cafeteria to find Emily and Vick, I can't help but sense a rise in the stakes, something yet to come. The image of a sweater being pulled apart by a single, loose thread pops into my head. But is that sweater mine or someone else's?

6

A complicated script had already been written and applied. With each run, the script works its magic. Essentially, each pass attempts to find holes in the wi-fi network - a back door.

Despite the urgency, the hacker sips on coffee and types with one hand to keep at it, altering the script as needed, screen capturing the log periodically. Every minute or so, they pull a cinnamon and coconut encrusted mini-donut from a box and pop it whole, then more coffee, still logging keystrokes with their free hand.

The motives for the attack are known only by a couple of people, the full story, of course, held closely by only one. The network breach serves to further the agenda of someone looking to control information, steer a narrative in a particular direction, and rouse a suspected and significant falsehood that could ruin lives, if not end them.

After some hours, successful entry is gained, the traffic data extracted for further analysis. Considerable effort is made to remove all traces of the foreign presence, then the encrypted data is forwarded through hidden channels to a completely anonymous smart phone. That data will be scrutinized. If suspicions are confirmed, a plan of action will lead to a reckoning.

Once the download is complete, a text message comes through from the receiving end.

'Any issues?'

'Not on my end. There is definitely something going on. The trace turned up some interesting things.'

'I look forward to seeing what you found.'

'If it means what I think it means, we have a serious problem.'

'One we'll deal with when the time is right. Please await further instructions.'

'Will do.'

7

With nervous steps, Emily enters the tech war room of AWT known as The Bridge. She finds Tisha and Marty sitting at their respective stations. Tisha continues working. Marty rises and comes over to greet Emily.

"Come on in. How have you been?"

The tension in Emily's shoulders eases some at the warm greeting. She meets Marty halfway to his desk and shakes his outstretched hand. Tisha is busy typing away at her computer but manages a quick wave that Emily reciprocates.

"Hey guys. Things are going okay. The usual hacker BS."

"God, I remember living at that house," Marty says. "It's had some serious upgrades since my time there, but damn, major cabin fever. Us Tech Ops people don't get to leave nearly as much as the gunslingers, so we get it real bad."

"Yes!" Emily agrees. "Thank you. Gunslingers. That's funny."

Tisha has stopped working and joins Emily and Marty at the head of the giant center console.

"Hey, if they get to call us nerds and geeks," Tisha says, "we get to use some nicknames too. I've been known to call them gravediggers, hospice workers. They get all riled up when you make fun of them. So sensitive."

They share a laugh. They're an exclusive club within the organization. Leaning on one another for support and understanding in their field is of critical benefit. Though most of the solo assassins become relatively proficient with some tech obstacles, no other people at AWT could do any Anonymous level hacking or script planting like the three of them. They hold a unique place in the world of contract assassination, a powerful one, perhaps more so than they even realize.

"I take it the latest mission went well?" Tisha asks. "I hear the guy tried to blow Josey up with a grenade."

"Tried and failed. Not much for me to do on that one, but yes, they got it done."

"Good," Marty says. "You guys are doing just fine. No news is good news."

"Any issues you've personally come across at the house or on the missions?" Tisha asks.

Whether it's real or perceived, Emily hears the question and sees it as a probe into her own recent discoveries at the house. For the briefest of moments, Emily thinks about spilling the beans, just to take the burden off her shoulders, even at the risk of seeming weak or incapable. But as quickly as the thought passes through her head, it runs the opposite way.

"Nothing I can think of."

"You sure? That's what we're here for, ya know. We're all on the same team. You can't expect to know everything."

"Pretty sure. But thank you. I appreciate that. I'll definitely keep that in mind."

"Okay," Tisha says. "Well, I have things to do, so I'm gonna get back to work. It was good to see you again."

"You too."

"Hey, you wanna get a coffee?" Marty asks. He turns around and walks back to his station to grab his thermal mug. "I need a refill."

"Sure," Emily responds. "I'm sure the rest of the team will be a little while, so I've got some time to kill."

"Be back shortly," Marty says to Tisha. "The bridge is yours."

8

It was a long day at headquarters, one that left me full of questions and even more dread. The three of us arrived back at the house with little conversation, all of us no doubt processing our interviews and psychological probings. Emily seemed especially distraught. She wouldn't even make eye contact with me on the way home or throughout the evening.

We are all now hiding out in our rooms for the night, which works out well for me. The rain stopped in the late afternoon and that means my plan to escape this evening is getting the greenlight.

I threw a few items in a backpack yesterday so I'd be ready to go in case we got back late. Not sure what I'll need, so I went with some basics: two small guns with extra clips, a change of clothes, four thousand dollars in cash, the phone Ollie gave me, a bottle of water, and a box of granola bars. I was anticipating a long journey on foot but that was before Ollie's gift. Now, I'll just hike a good distance away, maybe five miles, then call a cab.

I tiptoe down the stairs with my bag over my shoulder. I'm dressed all in black with a hoodie under my jacket. I have the hood down for now. I don't want to raise suspicions in case anyone is watching. My blind spots are all outside.

I exit the house via the rear kitchen door. There's a patio set on the deck we often use to eat outside when Vick grills. I take a seat near the far corner and stare out into the darkness. I don't know what I hope to find out by returning to the Randallstown Children's Home, the place I spent ten years of my childhood after my parents disappeared. I have no knowledge of who they were, the kind of people they might have been, or what happened to them. As far as I know, no one does. Ollie has left me doubting everything I've been told, which wasn't much to begin with. A quick internet search I did last night for someone named Allister Cole in the Baltimore area has turned up nil. I'll ask around and hopefully figure something out, or else my curiosity for the truth is going to make my head explode.

Fifteen minutes pass and I finally have the nerve to take off. I walk down the steps of the deck, and in one smooth motion, flip my hood up and drop to my hands and knees. I crawl for two hundred feet along an imaginary line I believe to be one of the blind spots Emily identified for me. The rain from earlier has left the ground muddy in spots but I slosh on. By the time I hit the fence, I'm filthy.

I had spent some time over the last four months, link by link, cutting a small hole in the fence to squeeze through. I push my bag through and then slither out myself. I rise, wanting desperately to change my clothes. I settle for taking off my jacket and tying it around my waste. With my bag over my shoulder, I head off. It's just after eleven o'clock and I have a long voyage ahead of me.

I walk through the wilderness for what I guess is about a mile before heading left to the road. I hop a short fence that is ten feet from the edge of the road. The brush is over a foot tall so it's difficult to walk through, but I stay in it near the fence in case I need to hide, should a car drive by. I doubt any will at this hour but I'll play it safe just the same.

I trudge along with a tiny LED flashlight aimed at the ground. I'd rather not step into a giant hole and bust my ankle, ending my little rendezvous. I've estimated it will take me an hour and a half to get five miles out. The tall grass slows my progress.

One hour and thirty-six minutes after I crawled through the fence, I reach the intersection of 225E Road and Route 21. I go right on Route 21 and walk five more minutes until I reach 210E Road. I lean up against the stop sign and use the phone Ollie gave me to arrange for an Uber. This is the one hiccup that might exist in my plan. I'm out in the middle of nowhere at about one a.m. and trying to call for a ride. It may look suspicious to many drivers, and thus, dangerous. My only other option is to walk for ten more miles and get to the next small town before getting a ride. I don't want to do that. There will be a much greater chance that someone will see me and I can't have that, not so close to home.

After twenty minutes, I finally get a confirmation from the app that someone is on their way to get me. Phew. I was getting worried.

Another twenty-two minutes later, a teal Prius arrives. I pull down my hoodie so they can get a look at me. I've got a little dirt on my pants but I'm a short woman. I doubt I come across as threatening.

A surprisingly large man for having such a tiny car exits the vehicle.

"You call for the ride?" he asks. The man is over six feet tall, stout, full red beard and head of hair, and he's wearing gray sweatpants, sneakers, and a zip-up navy-blue hoodie. I'm thinking I should probably be the fearful one here. This guy's a woodcutter's axe away from being right out of the latest Hollywood teenage massacre movie. Then again, I'm kind of bad-ass right now, so I'm betting I can take him.

"I did. Thank you so much for accepting."

"So, you're Samantha? Are you okay? You look like you've been crawling around in mud."

"Yep, that's me. And you have no idea. I just ... had a situation I needed to get away from. I'm okay though, thank you."

"I'm Mark. Go ahead and hop in the back and we'll be on our way."

"Awesome."

The interior of the car is more spacious than I expected. I place my bag next to me and take a moment to rifle through it, one last check to make sure I have everything I need.

"You got someone in Binghamton? Somewhere to go?"

"I'm taking a bus into the big city. Got friends there."

"That's good. NYC ... not my cup of tea but people seem to like it."

"It's a nice place to visit. I wouldn't want to live there. Too noisy for me."

I let him believe I'm going to New York City. I'm actually heading to Baltimore. My plan is to catch the 4:45 a.m. bus from Binghamton to Scranton, Scranton to Philly, then one final bus to Baltimore. Once there, I'll get a car so I can bounce around easier without detection. I'll have my temptations when I return, I know that, but my true mission is to drive over to Randallstown and pay a visit to Rosemary Greenburg, the woman who runs the orphanage I once called home. She was unbearably hard-assed and unforgiving, at least to me, so part of me holds some trepidation at the idea of seeing her, but another part of me, the now fully functioning adult who just happens to be an assassin, isn't worried. I could end her life in three seconds, yet the little girl inside of me is still fearful, all rumbling with anxiety at the mere prospect of speaking with her again.

Outside of plucking her for information about how I came to be at her children's home and who I really am, I cannot conceive of any words I would say to her. To me, she defined the idea of a wicked stepmother - rigid and cruel.

We arrive ninety minutes later to dead early morning streets. I tip the driver an extra hundred bucks for taking a chance on me and forgetting that he ever saw me. He attempts to refuse but I don't take NO for an answer.

"Be safe. And good luck," he says.

I nod, smile, and get out. I hang out in the shadows of the west side of the bus depot until it's time to go.

All the bus transfers went smoothly. When I stepped off

the final bus on the near east side of Baltimore, it was like I had been on a long vacation and was finally returning home, except this isn't my home anymore, and I'm sure as hell not on any vacation.

I take a taxi to Bill Wesson's Auto Ranch, my long standing favorite car dealer. I called Hank, the salesman I used to deal with, while on the bus ride between Scranton and Philadelphia. He said he'd be working until nine p.m., so as long as I got in before then, we could do business.

I arrive at fifteen to nine. The damn place hasn't changed a single iota since I last came. Hank, on the other hand, stopped fighting his male-pattern baldness and just resigned to shaving his head. He actually looks better this way.

"Been a while, Jo. I've missed your frequent visits. How's my best customer been? Or more like, where have you been?"

"Busy. I've been very, very busy. Glad to be back, though it'll be short lived. I'm tired. Been on the road all day, so if you don't mind, let's check out that Malibu you suggested on the phone."

"Right down to business. You haven't changed a bit. It's right there." Hank points to his right.

The burgundy 2005 four-door is a little beat up but Hank assured me it runs just fine. We walk over to it together. I pull open the driver's side door and hop in. The keys are in the ignition.

"Ninety-eight thousand miles but taken care of. The body condition is about typical for something twelve years old on the east coast."

"Thanks, Hank. You've always been good to me. I'll take it. How much?"

"Well, I thought about that. How sure are you that you'll be selling it right back to me a few days?"

"One hundred percent positive. Why?"

"If you promise me you'll bring it back, I'll just let you borrow it, say ... for five hundred bucks. No paperwork, no nothing. I don't take a full lot inventory for five more days, so no one will miss it. I've already put some dealer plates on it."

"Wow, Hank. You'd do that for me?"

"Only you. You've bought a shit ton of cars from me over the years. Just park it next to the building after close and leave the keys in the glove box."

I get out of the car and give Hank a hug. Not my usual style, but this is a big favor and he looks like he needs a hug.

"Thank you. I won't forget it."

"No sweat."

I turn around so Hank can't see what I'm doing and unzip my bag. I remove five one hundred-dollar bills, close the bag, and turn back around.

"Here you go then." I hand him the money.

"Pleasure doing business with you. Whatever it is you're doing back in Baltimore, try not to get yourself hurt. The world's a helluva lot more interesting with you in it."

I smile. "I appreciate that. I'll drop it off in a couple of days. I do gotta run." I pat him on the arm and get back in the car.

He waves me off and I speed away to my next destination.

I drive the streets of Baltimore and lose all track of time. The familiarity gives me comfort. The whirlwind events of the last year or so have me nostalgic and longing for a time when my life was simpler, not that it was ever all that simple. For tonight, at least, I'm free of prying eyes and accountability, so I'm taking advantage of it with a long, quiet drive. I know where I need to go, but for now, I'm just driving with no destination in mind.

When I finally stop, my eyes are heavy from exhaustion. I look over to my left and realize I'm parked outside the Leer house with no memory of coming here. Somehow, my wandering and subconscious mind drew me to this side of town.

The house is dark. It's after ten so that's not really much of a surprise. I glance over to the passenger seat just for reassurance that my bag is still there. I've placed three thousand dollars in a paper lunch sack, per the usual, for the Leer family. They haven't received so much as a text message from me since the day I completed my second final exam mission. I hope they don't feel like I've abandoned them. In my new line of work, I may never again be able to spend time with them, but I sure as hell will continue to look after them. One day, perhaps after I've accumulated some serious assassin's wealth and retired, we'll be able to live again as civilized and people no longer under threat. Something to wish for and a goal to reach.

With the paper sack in hand, I quietly leave my car, looking up and down the street, and trot across, around the side of the house and into the backyard. I scale the deck steps to an exterior door that leads through a pantry and into the kitchen. I pull a lock-picking kit from my back pocket and use two long, thin metal prongs to open the door. The only light is from the stovetop clock, glaring bright LED white. The place still smells like the tuna casserole they must have had for dinner. I pop open the fridge and steal a can of some generic lemon-lime soda. I take a seat at the island and put the money bag on the counter.

As slow as I can, I pop open the soda and guzzle about half of it. I put the can down and stare at the paper sack. I wrote 'From Me' on the bag. There's a note inside with words to the effect of missing them, hoping things are going well, can't wait for the day I can see them again. What I truly want is for Evie to come screaming down those stairs and damn near tackle me. I know the danger is too great. Hell, just being here could be a problem. One never knows who is watching.

I need to head out before I fall asleep right here in the kitchen. Wouldn't they shit a brick when they came down in the morning to find me snoozing. Alas, not going to happen. I have a seedy, cash-only motel in mind to stay at tonight. Tomorrow, I'll drive over to Randallstown and do what I'm here to do: visit the children's home I spent the better part of ten years at and question Rosemary Greenberg. This time, I won't be a scared and rebellious teen, but a grown-ass woman with a license to kill. Knowing this provides little comfort or confidence.

I leave the house undetected and drive away. It takes me about thirty minutes to reach The Motel on the far west side of town. Not the cleverest name but whatever. I picked it out ahead of time as it seemed like the closest spot on the way to Randallstown without actually being there.

I pull into the half-gravel, half torn up asphalt parking lot and right up to the only space available on the office end of the long building. I take my bag with me, which is currently doubling as my wallet, and enter the glass and metal door with a ringing from above my head. I don't see anyone but can hear a television playing out of sight. Suddenly, the TV goes mute and through a doorway behind the desk emerges a pudgy and slovenly woman maybe in her fifties. She could be in her forties. I've noticed that people living hard lives or that generally don't take care of themselves always seem older than they actually are. I'm betting she's one or both of these. As she approaches the counter, there's an overwhelming cloud of cigarette smoke and the faint smell of bologna.

The woman gives me a confused stare through squinted eyes, then she clears her throat. "You lost kid?" Her voice is raspy from three packs a day. It's obvious I'm not her usual clientele. I was able to clean up a bit at one of the bus station bathrooms at least. The mud I once had on my clothes might have helped me fit in better.

I raise an eyebrow and say nothing.

She itches her neck and lowest chin. "Sure you ain't wanting the Hilton?" She clears her throat again. "It's 'bout ten miles up the road heading east," she points.

I reach in my bag and pull out two, crisp one hundred-dollar bills and place them flat on the counter, removing my hand to make sure she can see them.

"I like it here. Two nights, no visitors, no questions."

She looks down at the money, then back up at me, then

down to the money again, then she puts her hands on the bills.

I firmly place my hand on hers but not aggressively so. "If anyone should come around here over the next couple of days or at any time in the future looking for someone like me, you've never seen any such person. Ok?"

She slides her hand out from under mine with the money and stuffs the bills into her bra. I can't help but think about how grateful I am she's wearing one. She turns and removes a key from the pegboard behind her and places it on the counter, sliding it over. "No one like you's ever stayed here. Number twelve, very end. Try not to trash the place."

"Thank you." I snatch the key and hurry out of the office, ready to crash for the night.

I pull my car around to the end of the building and use the key to enter my room. I close the door behind and lock it. I should be safe for the night, or at least I keep telling myself. I don't even bother turning on a light to check out the room. I throw my bag on the right side of the double bed, remove my pants, top, and shoes, and fall face down onto the mattress. It's as uncomfortable as I imagined it would be but it doesn't matter. Within a few minutes, I'll be out.

My eyes finally open at seven-thirty. A tiny bit of light is trying to creep around the drapes of the lone window. I can't remember the last time I slept eight hours without waking up. Maybe this is the first time in a long while I've not been on red alert. Even at the Kill House, I'm not always relaxed. I can imagine that in my new line of work these moments will be rare. I just wish those hours could have been spent getting room service at that Hilton the stinky motel lady mentioned. Oh well. I don't plan on being in this room except to sleep. Now, I need a fucking shower and the biggest coffee I can get my hands on.

I turn on the end table lamp and get my first good look at the room. Not half as bad as I thought it would be. Outdated furniture, check. Tube TV with digital converter, check.

Carpet worn down by ninety percent, check. Gold light fixture hanging by a chain over a round table in the corner, check. But it's not as filthy as I expected and I haven't seen a cockroach yet. Granted, I'm not going to bust out a black light and get the real truth. No thanks. Don't need that right now.

I hit the bathroom, pee, and get a good look in the mirror. My hair has managed to kink up to the left a bit. If I had some smearing lipstick and wonky mascara, I'd be ready for a good old-fashioned early morning walk of shame, minus the sex. Fortunately, I'm just a truant assassin who crawled through a fence in the mud, spent most of the day on a bus, and ended up in a seedy motel. I don't always make great life choices, but when I do ... oh wait, I don't.

I move to the shower and turn the water on full to the left. It won't be as hot as I'm used to but that's okay. I'll only be in there long enough to get the Greyhound off me.

As the water cascades over my head and body, I can't help but think about my parents. I know nothing about them. Not what they looked like, where they worked, if they were good or bad people, if they loved me. I have some illusive, gut feeling I'm not going to like what I find, should I get lucky enough to uncover anything.

Whatever happened to them has been hidden from me, that I can be sure of. On the bus rides over, I managed to do a few internet searches that yielded absolutely nothing. Allister Cole, the name Ollie gave me, came up a big blank. Without knowing what or where that name may be applicable, I couldn't narrow down anything. I searched my full name and sometimes just my last name in and around the Baltimore area. That was also fruitless. There isn't even a local record of a Josey Baldwin being born around here during the time I believe I was born. Either I'm not from these parts or Josey Baldwin isn't my given name, maybe both. My birth certificate could be a forgery, and with that, even my birthdate could have been altered. I started to feel like I was on a wild goose chase.

Regardless of my failed internet research, I've always figured I would have the best chance of getting some information by just talking directly to Dr. Greenberg. If anyone had even a snippet of information, it'd be her. She was at Randallstown when I arrived and was there when I ran away. If there have been secrets kept about me, I can't imagine why she couldn't be forthcoming about my past now. I haven't been around there in like a decade. I'm all grown up and a woman of the world. Then again, in the world I live in now, things are rarely as they seem, with often a darker truth hiding behind every locked door.

I leave nothing behind in the room as I set off this morning. I backtrack five miles toward Baltimore to pick up a coffee before heading back towards Randallstown. The caffeine brings me to life in the most pleasant way. Somehow, my mood is even light, especially considering the face to face I'm about to have.

Not much has changed about Randallstown since I left. There's a gas station where the chicken place used to be, minor differences like that. The houses and streets and general atmosphere seem about the same. I get no sense of dread, no impending doom, no ill will. Quite frankly, I feel like a stranger coming back here. I recognize the place, but it's almost like I've only seen it in pictures and this is my first time here in person. It's strange.

Muscle memory takes me straight to the parking lot of my destination. I park and exit the car, my bag with me at all times. The grass is green, the trees rustling in a peaceful breeze. I can hear children laughing and shouting in the distance. I'm put at ease as I walk to the front door. I think I expected to find a hell-gate here, fully equipped with demon tour guides and lava-filled flame spouts.

The building is gray stone and brick with a green roof. Outside of the modern windows, the architecture still speaks to its age. If I remember correctly, it was built in the late 1800s, originally as an off-site medical training facility for a local university. At some point in the 1950s, it became too antiquated for modern medicine, so it was sold to the state to be used as a children's home.

I pull open the large wooden door and step inside. The giant double-wide staircase straight ahead dominates the foyer. It's quiet. Not sure how many kids are currently living here, but then again, it's a school day, so there wouldn't be a lot of them around this time of day.

The first door on the right is reception. I open it and walk through as a few memories float around in my head. I take a deep breath and approach the desk. A woman not much older than me sits behind it, busy typing at a computer.

We make eye contact and I smile.

"Hello," I say.

"Hi. What can I do for you?"

"Well, um, actually, I'm here to see Dr. Greenberg. I spent some time here in my youth. Is she available?"

"Oh ... I'm sorry. Dr. Greenberg is no longer with us." There's a sadness in her eyes and in her voice.

"No longer with us?"

She shakes her head. "She passed away about ten months ago. I'm terribly sorry."

"Wow. Um. I'm little surprised. Do you happen to know how she died?"

"Natural causes, not sure beyond that. They found her in her kitchen."

I nod. Rosemary had to be in her sixties, so I guess I shouldn't be too surprised, but the timing seems weird. I mean, what are the odds that she would pass away right around the time I graduated the Kill Academy. I'm always suspicious of coincidence. That could just be the paranoid part of me talking, or the training. Either way, it's strange.

"So, were you close to Dr. Greenberg?" the woman asks.

"Was anybody? She could be ... difficult. I assume you knew her?"

"I did. I've been here for three years. And yes, I suppose she could be a bit of pill at times. So, you lived here? That had to be crazy."

"Oh yeah, it was a real hoot. But it's been like ten years since I left. Damn. I was really hoping to get some information from her."

"Is there anything I could help with? Or maybe our new director could?"

"I doubt it. It was kind of personal stuff. Was she still living over on Grover Street when she passed?"

"Oh yeah. The house ended up being sold at auction eventually."

"I see."

"I'm sorry. I hope you didn't travel too far to visit. It's been a while since the first one, but you're actually the second person who stopped by that didn't know she passed."

My mind is turning, unsure what to do or where to go next to get answers. This is going to end up being a waste of time. The receptionist's words finally unfold in my ear.

"Not far. Thank you. The other person that stopped by, when was that?"

"Not long after she passed."

"You remember what they looked like?"

"Tall black guy, stunningly deep voice. Looked like a lawyer or something."

Fuck. And the plot thickens.

"You wouldn't happen to be familiar with a guy named Allister Cole?"

"I don't think so, no. I'd remember that name."

Double dead end. I have to go get my head straight.

"Thank you again. You've been very helpful." I pat the edge of her desk and walk off before she can continue the conversation.

I fight the temptation to walk the hallways and dive further into my past. I leave the building the way I came in. Once in the car, I take a deep breath and ponder the development.

I come to the realization that both angles I had to get information have fizzled out pretty fast but a new trail has emerged. I've found nothing on Allister Cole, and now

Rosemary has given me nothing. I'm growing tired of the cryptic bullshit surrounding my past. Clearly, Ollie knows something, so I need him to just cut the crap and tell me. Maybe he'll meet me this evening, away from the eyes and ears of the company.

I pull out the phone Ollie gave me and send him a text.

'I feel like I'm on a wild goose chase. Can u meet me 2nite?'

'That's risky'

'I know. Haven't been able to come up with jack-shit on the YOU KNOW WHAT'

'Give me a sec'

...

'Ok. I can drive up to the house after 3'

'Ummm ... yeah ... I'm not exactly at the house'

'Ok. Where r u?'

'Baltimore. Randallstown more precisely'

'Jesus! If you get caught...'

'I know. I had to get away, do some in-person research'

'Where should we meet?'

'There's an abandoned school on Miller, 2 miles off Main in Randallstown. Back parking lot'

'I'll be there in a black SUV at 7 o'clock'

'Thank u'

'When we're done, u need to get ur ass back home'

'I will'

Mentally, I'm exhausted. To wind down, I drive around town a little, swinging by each of the spots I used to frequent. I stop by the high school I attended only freshmen year. After running away from Randallstown and Dr. Greenberg, my classroom days were done. I feel some sort of way about that from time to time, not finishing high school, though I can't quantify how or why it matters. I suppose there's a social stigma attached to high school dropouts, but I exist in the mirror version of reality, where no one ever mentions diplomas and degrees. We talk dime-bags and dollars. In the normal world, people talk about their suburban houses, their hybrid cars, and their corporate careers. Here in the mirror world, it's more like crack houses, SUVs with tinted windows, and corporate espionage. When you make a mistake at that corporate job, you might get a firm talking-to. Out here, you might just get a firm crack to the dome with the butt of a gun.

There might be a small part of me that regrets a few of my choices. Would I be better off? Happier? No idea. There really isn't much point in lingering there. I am where I am. Can't move backward.

From the outside of the high school, nothing has changed, like someone took a picture and said, 'Let's keep it exactly like this forever.' I sit for a few minutes and try to remember my days here. My time at school was my only real escape from the children's home, yet I have no lasting memories, good or bad. I have mental images of the people, places, and things from my freshman year but they lack emotional attachments. It's like I was in a meditative state the whole time, floating through time to keep myself sane. If only I could've kept that state of being while at the Home.

The shopping center where all the kids would hang out after school is still there too, though many of the businesses are different. The east end of it had a convenience store we'd buy candy and soda from, and it's still around, only different in name. I recall a group of us hanging out once behind the building, passing around a bottle of whiskey, some smoking cigarettes, others weed. I imbibed but left the smoking for others. I can see now that it was then I developed my taste for the hard, brown liquors.

I pop in to pick up some snacks and a cold coffee. It's cleaner than I remember, and brighter, different enough that I get no instant nostalgia. When I checkout, the clerk is a friendly older gentleman that smiles wide. I pay with cash and leave in a better mood than when I came in.

As I approach the exit, I see a woman getting into her car

- long, graying hair, tweed skirt, white blouse. She reminds me of Dr. Greenberg. I have no fond memories of her. My last encounter was no different, but it led me out of Randallstown and into the life I'm living now.

9

About ten years ago

I had found and swiped an old duffel bag from the laundry room the night before. I managed to stuff a few outfits in, a flashlight I stole from the janitor, a bunch of cereal bars I'd been hoarding from snack time, and a Swiss Army Knife Casey Littleton had traded me for a hand job. I wasn't sure how I'd survive on my own, I just knew I could no longer be there.

After a little incident with Dr. Greenberg, I had no other choice but to bail. I didn't think I could stand one more day in that hellhole. She had always treated me differently than the other kids, at least as far back as I could remember. I never knew why, and I didn't care anymore. I had to get out. My plan to escape had started three weeks prior.

I was never good enough for her and I could never do anything right, or at least that's how she made me feel. Whenever us orphans acted out, we were punished, often severely. Rosemary's iron fist, when it came down, came down hard. We'd lose TV, gaming, and computer privileges, bedtime snacks, outdoor time. Those may seem like trivial things, but to an orphaned teenager at a hard knocks children's home, they were often everything. We'd gain extra kitchen duties (mostly doing the dishes), be forced to use an old toothbrush to scrub the basemoulding in every hallway, get weed-pulling and snow-shoveling duty when the season fit, and end up with any number of other tiny tortures she would devise to steal away our self-respect and dignity.

Somehow, perhaps because of my own behavior, but mostly because Rosemary had it out for me, I found myself being punished ten times more often than any other child at the facility. The specific incident that brought about my urge to finally leave came when myself and three other kids, all boys, snuck out one night to hide behind the tool shed to smoke and drink and just to hang out without supervision.

During a bed inspection, Rosemary discovered the four of us missing, our usual trick of putting pillows under the blankets to look like bodies failing miserably. She had been informed by the groundskeeper that kids were hanging out behind the shed. He kept finding cigarette butts and empty beer bottles, and got tired of picking up after our messes.

In the dark and without a flashlight, she stormed out of the building and across the yard.

"What in the hell do you all think you're doing out here?" she screamed, scaring the crap out of us. We made failed attempts to hide the alcohol and snuff out the smokes.

We all got to our feet but said nothing in rebuttal. The boys stood in shame, their heads bowed, hands at their sides. I used no such body language. My shoulders slumped, I sighed in annoyance, pissed off that our momentary freedom had ended, and most definitely not fearful we had been caught.

Rosemary shook her head in disappointment. "I just don't know what to do with you idiots. You must think I'm stupid, clearly." She looked me dead in the eye and sneered. "Pick up your damn garbage and get back to your rooms immediately. We'll discuss your punishments tomorrow."

The guys picked everything up and headed past Rosemary on their way back in. I began to follow but was halted by her outreached arm.

"I know what you're up to out here. If you want to be a little slut, you can wait and do it when you're out of my care. This behavior you're engaging in stops now!"

I had no idea what she was referring to. Up to that point, I hadn't done anything sexual in my time there. I guess she assumed that the fact I always hung out with guys and not girls, I must be fucking them. It wasn't true, not even close. I was a tomboy and simply preferred the company of males.

"Whatever." I refused to even acknowledge her accusations with a denial.

"You're such a smartass. If you were my daughter, I'd slap the shit out of you."

"Oh, I wish you would," I said.

"I wouldn't give you the pleasure you little snot. I wouldn't dare throw my career away over a little bitch like you."

I walked away without another word. I didn't want to hear her voice, grating on my ears like truck brakes badly in need of being replaced. And I sure as hell didn't want her to see how infuriated she had made me.

The next morning, I awoke to find the door to my room locked. I was pissed. I pounded on the door for five minutes before Alexis, Rosemary's assistant, came to let me out. I chewed her ass out. It was a Saturday, so Rosemary wouldn't be in that day. When I found out the boys got their computer privileges taken away for the weekend and mine would be taken away for a month, I held back my fury for the unfairness of the punishment, as the plans for my eventual escape stewed within.

Three weeks later, after the main staff had left for the day, I gathered my things, opened the window in my room, and climbed out. When I hit the sidewalk, I turned and looked back at the building, flames and hate in my eyes and heart. I walked on, hitched a ride to Baltimore, and until now, had never returned.

Those early days on the streets of Baltimore were hard. I couldn't use my real name, I couldn't say a word about where I was from, and I had to change my looks and hide my face so as not to get recognized as the missing orphan reported on the news. I went Britney Spears crazy with a buzzed haircut, dyed it blonde, and with little breast development, I passed as a male named Joey Biscuits for about a year. Once the heat died down over the missing Josey Baldwin, I stopped dying my hair and let it grow out, eventually regaining my real identity.

This change couldn't have come at a better time either, because as Joey, I had used up all my street lives, burned all my low-life bridges, and milked all the charity I could gather. As a young woman, new again to the city, with no contacts and no enemies, I began to fine-tune my survival skills. I picked fights with weaker males and learned to defend myself, although, there were some close calls in the beginning.

I soon found myself in dark alleys where bad people did bad things. I listened, I learned, I studied patterns, and eventually, I worked up the courage to intercept a small-time dealer to steal his money after he received payment from his distributors.

The rush of that heist, the two thousand dollars in cash, all of it, lead me to believe I could do that forever. I wasn't quite seventeen years old by that point. I was small and had no trouble being invisible. That was my biggest asset, and really the only thing I could count on in those days. It would be several more years before I honed my fighting skills. Meeting Tom Sake turned out to be the best thing that ever happened to me in that department.

10

The black SUV is parked exactly where I told Ollie to be - in the rear parking lot of an abandoned middle school. It's seven p.m., so there aren't a lot of people on the streets. There's housing nearby, some shopping, restaurants, and a few coffee shops. The lot is quiet, equipped with crumbling concrete, faded parking lines, and only one working lamppost.

I parked several blocks away and walked from there. I approach the vehicle from the front so they are fully aware of my presence. Good way to get shot in my world, sneaking up on people. I'm wearing a hoodie and it's obscuring my face. I don't want Ollie's driver to recognize me, though it's unlikely he would even know who I am.

The passenger side rear door opens as I get close. I smile when I see Ollie.

"Hop in," he says.

I do and close the door behind me. "How are you?"

"Oh, it's been a whirlwind lately. Lot going on."

Careful to keep my face hidden, I address the driver, "Hey bud, there's a place just around the corner, why don't you go get a coffee or something?"

The guy looks into the rearview mirror and all matter of fact states, "I don't drink coffee."

Is this asshole really that dense? Wow.

"Yo, homey, I don't care where you fuckin' go, I just want you outta this SUV. Now hit the fuckin' road."

62

The guy whips his head around as if he's really going to challenge me, then he sees Ollie's face.

"Boss?"

Ollie reaches around and pulls his wallet from a back pocket, removes a twenty-dollar bill, and hands it to the driver. "Just take a walk, grab a drink or something. Come back in thirty minutes or so."

I look to Ollie and give him a couple of quick eyebrow raises, then look to the driver. "Make it an hour," I say.

The driver gives me a smart-ass look and I raise the back of my hand to threaten him.

"Fine." He snatches the money and leaves the vehicle.

I pull my hood back and turn slightly toward Ollie.

"Do I need to worry about him snitching on me?"

"Who, Mike? No. He's my personal driver and loyal to me. We're fine."

"Okay, good."

"So, what's really up?" Ollie asks. "It's a little unorthodox for us to be meeting like this."

"Hey! You started this shit with me," I say playfully.

"True."

"Well, I finally slipped away and had a little trip down amnesia lane here in Randallstown. Ever been here, aside from right now?"

"Maybe drove through here once."

"Funny thing, the lady running the front desk of the children's home here thought it was weird that for the second time in ten months, someone came by asking about Rosemary Greenburg that didn't know she had passed."

"Okay."

Ollie's poker face is steely. "When I asked her about the other person, she was quite clear about the very tall black man, shaved head, deep voice. Sound familiar?"

Ollie chuckles. "I have to give it to ya. You've got your head on a swivel. Good to hear, but if I were you, I'd be careful approaching people within the organization about things like this. Even me. I really don't know who can be trusted around there anymore."

"Yeah, but you're the one that started me down this path. You didn't kill her, did you?"

"No, I did not, but..." Ollie pauses, tilting his head. "I have some suspicions. The timing has me thinking."

"They say she died of natural causes. Do you think she was killed, and if so, to cover up something about me?"

"Simple answer, yes and yes."

"Shit. What the hell is going on, Ollie? You have to give me something. I'm flying blind here and getting paranoid. I just started diving into this crap and I've already found out someone is dead. When I look deeper into Allister Cole, am I going to find he's dead too?"

He gives me a peculiar look. "Well, Allister Coal is not a man, so no, he won't end up dead."

"Okay, now you're just fucking with me."

"Since time is not on our side here, I'm just going to steer you on this. I'm putting my own life at risk discussing this with you. I hope you can appreciate that."

"I do. I really do. Please. What the hell is going on?"

Ollie releases a troubling sigh. "You were close to getting bounced from the academy. That last mission, the one in Baltimore, was rigged to help you succeed at the behest of Madame K."

"I knew it!"

Ollie puts his right hand up. "Let me finish and then we can discuss it."

I nod. "Sorry."

"Dina and I both objected but were over-ruled. The org has never done anything like that before, and I don't consider it an acceptable way to do business. That was one of a few things that had been troubling some of us about Madame K in recent years. The fact that she was prepared to rig a mission just to get you into this job made me suspicious of her motives, so I started looking into it.

"That led me to Baltimore, to Randallstown, and ultimately to Allister Coal, the large coal mining operation in western Pennsylvania. I haven't had time to dig around in the coal company yet. I figured you could take it from here. Help me stay away from this mess for a while."

"Wow. I don't know what to say or what any of this means. Why does Madame K give a shit either way about me?"

"That's what we're trying to figure out."

"So, what led you to Allister Coal?"

"I searched Rosemary's home, which oddly enough was still just sitting there with all her shit, like it had been abandoned. She had no heirs and the state was dragging their feet with the estate stuff. Pretty sloppy work from whomever had her killed. I would have torched the house. Anyway, in her nightstand, I found the stub of a one-way airline ticket to Pittsburgh."

"Okay. What does that mean?"

"Someone had written on the back of it. April 14th, 2pm at Gil's Dinner, Route 8 near Hampton. That didn't seem odd but what really got me thinking was the date on the airline stub. This was three days before you were registered for the first time at Randallstown Children's home. Coincidence? Tell me, Josey. What do you know about your parents and where you came from?"

"I don't know anything. I was told they disappeared and were presumed dead. I've always assumed I came from the Baltimore area but I've never really looked into it. Never saw a reason to. In all honesty, I've been so bitter about being orphaned, I wanted nothing to do with that past. It's too painful. I was like five years old anyway."

"I did some minor poking around through the news in the Pittsburgh area for the days before you ended up in Rosemary's care, and it turns out, there was a husband, a wife, and a five-year-old child that disappeared, never to be found. The parents both worked at Allister Coal."

"So, what's so special about the coal company?"

"Nothing, on the surface, but I kept getting a weird feeling, so I dug around in the AWT archives and found a contract. This was before my time at the organization, so."

I feel my heart sink from my chest to my stomach as the meaning of the words decipher themselves. I look away, rub my forehead. The words gone-gone come to mind. Fuck. Is this really happening? Could this be true?

"Apparently, a woman named Anzu 'Annie' Jones, overheard a private conversation at Allister Coal, a real whistleblower type situation. Whatever it was, it must have been pretty bad. When she came forward with the knowledge, a contract for her life was taken out. Apparently, her entire family was ghosted."

"Oh, Jesus Christ!" I try to process all the implications of this news but just can't wrap my head around it. Suddenly, all the puzzle pieces fall into place for me. Was Annie my mother? Oh Christ. "Why is this happening to me?" I'm ready to pull my hair out, and honestly, I might just cry.

"I'm really sorry, Josey." Ollie places his hand on my hand. "I can't imagine how you must feel. This is really fucked up."

I move the palm of my hand to the palm of his. Our fingers fold together, gently. A single tear runs down my left cheek. We release our clasped hands and he brings one up to wipe the moisture from my face. I've never seen this side of Ollie. It makes me want him even more.

I aggressively grab his wrist and make him doubt my intentions for an instant, but then I look him in the eyes before kissing the side of his pinky finger.

"Josey, we have to be really careful here. Our lives are in danger."

I shake my head. "Later. Right now, I want you." I kiss the top of his hand. "I don't wanna think about anything else."

11

Ten months ago

Dr. Rosemary Greenburg arrived at home that Friday like all others: worn out, physically and mentally. The house was a well-kept mid-sixties brick ranch she inherited from her father, Quentin, after he suffered a massive heart attack that killed him instantly. She barely spoke to him despite living in the same town. Rosemary could never live up to the example her mother, Gladys, had set before being killed in a car accident when Rosemary was just twelve years old. She and her mother fought constantly, mostly because Rosemary could never be taught to control her mouth. When she disagreed, she expressed it. When she found fundamental flaws in something, she couldn't help but voice her opinion. Her parents quickly grew weary of Rosemary's inability to accept simple answers. They were simple people, after all, but their daughter's intellect could not be contained. The rift followed both parents to their graves.

Quentin never outright blamed Rosemary for Gladys' death, as it simply wasn't true, but he made every effort to make Rosemary feel as if it were. He never wasted an opportunity to remind her how wonderful a woman Gladys had been, and how Rosemary would never be as beautiful and kind and generous as her mother. For Rosemary, the bitterness and resentment built up for years, becoming a huge part of her natural demeanor and personality, and that combined with her snarky and often brutally truthful tongue, left her hard to employ, and even harder to love.

She'd been in charge of the Randallstown Children's Home since just after turning thirty. At sixty-two years old though, her many years of fighting the constant battles of institutional bureaucracy, the defiant at-risk youth of the Greater Baltimore area, and her own career and personal demons, had left her appearance and soul aged by what felt like two extra decades.

She had a knack for knowing what people were thinking and why, so her pursuits in social work, specifically child psychology and sociology made perfect sense. She graduated with top honors and found work quickly in her field of choice, but her inability to handle interpersonal relationships eventually left her unemployed and perpetually single. Only a desperate and tearful phone call to her former doctoral advisor from the university yielded anything on the job front. Dr. Talbot knew of a position opening soon that might better suit her skills and personality, one that would have her in charge of only a few adults with much lesser degrees than her own, or none at all, and mostly working with children. She seized the opportunity and never looked back.

Like every day after getting home, Rosemary went straight to her bedroom, kicked the navy-blue flats off her feet, rolled the knee-high panty hose from her legs, then slid into the house slippers she had carefully placed at the end of her bed.

From there, she hit the kitchen to make a chia tea and pre-heat the oven for a dinner of leftover lasagna. She flipped through the seven junk mail envelopes and two catalogs while sipping on her mug until the oven beeped. She placed the food on the center rack, set the timer for twenty-five minutes, and with her drink in hand, started to head to the living room.

Rosemary jerked in alarm as she turned to leave, her feet coming off the ground, the mug of tea flying from her hand and crashing to the ceramic tile floor some five feet away. An uninvited guest stood in the archway.

"What the hell are you doing in my house?" Rosemary said. When she looked at the intruder, there was a familiarity in the person's eyes she couldn't place.

"These twenty years have not been kind to you, Dr. Greenburg." The intruder pulled back the hood from their head, revealing their identity.

"Well, you've barely changed at all." Rosemary relaxed somewhat, despite the fact she knew the visit was bound to be unpleasant. "I somehow knew you'd be back one day. You make a deal with the devil, the debt always come due."

"Unfortunately, that is truer than I would like to admit."

"So, don't leave me in suspense. What exactly are you here for?" With her feet on fire from standing half the day, Rosemary slowly pulled a stool away from the counter and sat down.

"To tie up a loose end. Time has caught up with us."

Rosemary swallowed hard at those words. "Do you know the risk I endured to take her in? It could have ended my career. Hell, I could've ended up in jail. Doesn't that mean anything to you? I did you a rather large favor."

"And I appreciate that, but I can't be bothered with balancing some imaginary scale anymore. For every life I've taken, I've probably saved hundreds, maybe thousands. I consider myself to have a sort of ... get out of jail free card. Besides, you were well compensated."

"Yeah, with money I could never really spend without suspicion. I have nothing to show for it."

"Those exotic trips you took overseas were far from nothing."

"How the hell do you know about...? Oh, Jesus. I don't want to know." Rosemary sighed. She closed her eyes. Moments from her life, mostly ones she had regret for, buzzed through her mind. She attempted to wipe them clean by recalling a happy time, even one of modest contentment, yet she failed. Sadness filled her heart as she settled into her fate. "Well, let's just get it over with. I'm too old and too tired and I just don't give a damn."

"It'll be painless, unlike the rest of your life has been. I'll at least do that for you."

"Your words mean nothing to..." Before she could finish her sentence, Rosemary felt a clench in her throat and lost her breath. She reached to her neck. Her eyes bulged ever so slightly. A pain hit her chest. Three second later, she slid off the stool and collapsed to the floor.

The intruder noted the time. The poison placed in the chia tea worked a few minutes faster than expected, probably due to the overall negative health of Rosemary. It will be undetected in her bloodwork, as it's a compound never tested for. The autopsy will show she had a heart attack, death by natural causes. No one that knew her would be surprised by that outcome.

The assassin left the house as it was, including the lasagna heating up in the oven, the chia tea mug shattered on the floor. Those details would lend believability to a sudden medical emergency in the home of a single, friendless woman. She died in much the way she always felt: alone, exhausted, and hopeless.

12

Unknown Location

An alert bell dings on the hacker's computer, notification that someone has fallen victim to the malware email plant. The hacker has put in place a way for every keystroke to now be recorded, but more importantly, first level access to the heavily secured network has been granted. The malware works quickly, silently, pinging servers, gathering information for later review.

After hours of incoming data, the hacker scans that data and doesn't find enough to satisfy. In fact, a second, even more well encrypted subset of servers is uncovered, offering what could be an insurmountable level of security. The hacker is experienced and seen their fair share of precautionary computer defense systems, but this one is at a level more akin to the federal government. The secrets hidden behind such a formidable firewall could potentially be worth millions of dollars, and certainly kill worthy.

The hacker has been assigned to do a job, one that has involved many months of preparation, hardship, surveillance, infiltration, and lies. The mountain appears to be impossible to climb at this point but they cannot quit. They must continue. The danger will now escalate. One slip could mean exposure. Exposure means a very permanent end.

13

Before heading back home, I returned the car to Wesson's. After that, I called the number for an ad on Craigslist where a guy was selling his Chevy Cavalier. Rusty as hell, tires will need replaced soon, but runs great - $400 cash only. I met him a block down from Wesson's and took the keys and the title and was on my way.

For a little additional stress relief to go along with my encounter with Ollie, I stopped by my favorite animal shelter to get some puppy kisses and a few kitten scratches. For an hour, I actually forgot why I had come back to Baltimore, that I was now a paid assassin, that my parents may have been killed by the organization I now work for, and that everything I think I know is likely, at best - muddy water, at worst - a mirage.

I got back to the town where I had originally been dropped off by the burly Uber guy Mark at the start of this excursion and hit him up for another ride, but really, I needed more than that. It's risky to use the same person, I know, but I got the distinct impression he's a standup guy and doesn't really give a shit what I'm doing so long as the money is right.

I recall him telling me he helps run a small goat farm with his father, and for extra money they built a storage facility with thirty of those fifteen by twenty-foot storage spaces with red garage doors they rent out for like a hundred dollars a month.

When he picked me up, I took a chance and showed him the shitty car I had bought. I told him I needed a place to store it for periodic use, and that I remembered him mentioning his storage business. He said he had two bays available, each of them one hundred twenty-five dollars a month or one hundred if paid a year in advance. I handed him fifteen hundred cash and a request for complete anonymity. He agreed.

I followed him to the shed, stored the car, and had him give me a ride back to the corner he had originally picked me up a few days ago. As a favor, he offered to give me a ride to and from the storage place to pick up and drop off my car, off the books. I put his cellphone number in the phone Ollie gave me so I could text him for a ride when needed. We then parted ways.

I stay just off the road, bag over my shoulder, a shoebox cradled under my right arm. The walk is quick and quiet. I'm anxious to get home. My current pace is a millisecond slower than the average suburban speed walker. Not a single vehicle passes on the way. Thank god. I have no desire to be on my hands and knees hiding in a ditch.

I reach the hole in the fence and crawl through, pushing the shoebox and my bag in first. I decide to take a chance and walk upright to the house, ignoring the cameras. Maybe no one is watching, or maybe no one will care. I reach the back porch and as far as I know, no alarm has been triggered. I guess I'm good.

It's now after midnight. I get in the house, grab a bottle of water, a small bowl, and a cup of milk from the kitchen before heading to my room. The house is dark, including Emily and Vick's rooms.

I throw my bag on the floor, place the shoebox on the bed, and the stuff from the kitchen on my nightstand. With elation, I remove the lid from the shoebox and find Ginger, my recently adopted orange kitten with white paws and a half white tail. She's had a long journey too and looks ready to come out and find a nice soft place to curl up and sleep.

I let her high step around on the bed for a few minutes while I rest and drink some water. It's been a long couple of days, physically and emotionally. Watching Ginger explore the ridges of the blankets and get her little claws stuck in the threads is cathartic.

I grab the bowl from my nightstand and pour a little milk into it. I present it to Ginger, holding it firm to keep it from spilling. She steps over and sniffs a few times before lapping up most of it. I have no supplies for Ginger. We weren't specifically told we couldn't have a pet at the house, though I'm sure it's a no-no. Tomorrow, when I put in my food and toiletries order for the week, I'll have them pick me up litter and a litter box, food, some toys, and a kitty bed. Not sure how they'll react, but too fucking bad. No going back now. I need this.

"You need to go potty?" I baby talk her. "You need to go potty? Come on." I get off the bed and rifle through my bag to find the folded-up newspaper I bought in Randallstown. I take it and the kitty into the bathroom and close the door behind me. I put Ginger on the floor and lay out two sheets of the newspaper.

I repeatedly point to the paper and place her on it, saying the word potty. At first, she's more curious about the smell of the paper and ink. After a minute, much to my delight, she squats and does her business.

"Good girl," I praise. "Good girl."

I remove the wet page, replace it with another one, and wait a couple more minutes to see if she needs to go number two. She gets bored and wanders around the bathroom, so I give up and open the door. She runs out of the door and prances around, sniffing everything.

I take the cotton blanket from my bed and fold it into a little bundle as a makeshift bed. I decide to wait and take a shower in the morning, so I strip down and put Ginger in the bed next to where I sleep. Once the light is off, we're both out fast.

I awake the next morning to a knock at my bedroom door. I get out of bed and slip on my robe.

"Come in."

The door opens to reveal Vick with a somewhat sour look on his face.

"Where the hell have you been?" Vick asks.

I had a feeling he'd be pissed about it. "Out."

Vick looks down to the ground. "What the hell is that?"

I look down too to find a little bit of cat poop on the floor about two feet in front of him.

From under the bed, Ginger pops out, walks over to me, and rubs against my leg.

"Jesus, Josey. You got a fuckin' cat? Seriously?"

"I'll clean up. Calm down."

"Is this why you snuck out? I can tell Emily knows, she just won't admit it."

"Not entirely. But this is why I didn't tell you."

"We're supposed to be a team, and we're not supposed to leave like that."

"Always the boy scout. Ya know, you don't always have to abide by every stupid rule. I had things I needed to take care of. I was careful.

"Well, forgive me if I don't trust you completely, but you're putting all of our lives at risk by pulling this shit. What if someone had followed you back?"

"No one did." I pick up Ginger and put her on the bed.

"But what if someone had?"

"I was careful. I'm not stupid."

"If I can't trust you, I can't work with you."

"That's a little dramatic." I ponder whether I should tell Vick what I've been up to. I know he's trustworthy, but when it comes to the organization, my guess is that he'd be loyal to them over me, which means loyal to Madame K.

Vick throws his hands up with a verbal puff.

"Look, I need to hit the treadmill this morning. Join me and I'll tell you what I was doing. It's important but I have to be careful who I share it with. You can trust me, Vick. Can I trust you?"

"You know the answer to that."

"Okay. Give me ten minutes and meet me in the exercise room."

"Fine." Vick turns and leaves, shutting the door behind him.

I was pretty much expecting that reaction from Vick, although, I still held out hope he'd be cool about it. I'm not one hundred percent sure I should tell him anything. The problem is, if I don't, he'll never let it go, and that could end up being a bigger problem on our missions. That trust thing is invaluable in that space. He's right when he says there is risk in what I did. That's not lost on me. Knowing what I know now, I feel it was definitely worth it, and I'm not sorry to admit, I'll be doing it again very soon when I make a trip up to Allister Coal. There are still answers out there and I'm going to find them. He's just going to have to understand that.

I get dressed in workout clothes - a black tank-top, black yoga pants, white quarter socks and sneakers. I clean up Ginger's little mess, feed her some more milk, and leave her in the room with the bathroom door open in case she remembers what the newspaper is for.

I head down the stairs and find Emily in the living room with her laptop. She's watching a PBS nature show while working on her computer.

"Hey," I announce.

Emily stops whatever she's doing on her laptop and uses the TV remote to mute it. "Hey. I heard Vick yelling. Everything okay?"

"Oh yeah. Pissed about my breakout. No biggie."

In a slight whisper, "He grilled me about it. I revealed nothing."

"I appreciate that. I'm gonna tell him, else his anger might become a liability on our next mission. Can't have that."

"No. No we can't. So, how'd it go?"

"Some interesting developments, that's for sure, but

there's more to do, so I'll have to go out at least one more time to verify a few things. I'll fill you in after that trip."

"Just be careful out there."

"I will. Thanks again for your help with the," I stop and mouth the words 'camera thingy'. "Gotta go work out. See you after that."

"Okay. Have fun."

I leave, grab a bottle of water from the kitchen, and head to the exercise room where I find Vick already running on one of the three treadmills. A nineties grunge channel is playing on the loudspeakers. Good. I do a few simple leg stretches and hop on the middle treadmill to his right.

I start slow to get warmed up. We don't say a word for almost five minutes. I'm not sure if I should start or if I should wait for him to speak. There's a little psychological game at play here. I can feel it. He wants me contrite. I'm not going to give him that. It would be a lie anyway. I'm not sorry. I do want him to understand, and that's why I've decided to tell him the truth.

"What do you know about my final training mission at the academy?" I finally ask.

"I don't know. Why?"

"It was in Baltimore and someone I know got mixed up in it."

"I knew about the Baltimore part. I didn't know about the other. Who?"

"Doesn't matter. The point is, I had suspicions that the organization rigged the mission so I would succeed, and in doing so, they put someone I care a great deal about in danger. A child, to be more specific."

Vick ups the speed on this treadmill and is really starting to sweat.

"That's a heavy accusation. Could have been a coincidence."

"Maybe. But then later I came into some information that suggests otherwise, something from my past. Information provided to me from someone within AWT, so I know it's valid. I had to do some research, away from prying eyes, and that's where I was the last few days."

A full two minutes pass without a response from Vick. He slows his treadmill down for a cool down walk.

"You gonna say anything?" I ask.

"Not sure what to say. I understand your need to look into the situation but you're not supposed to leave the house without approval."

"It's pretty serious."

"I just don't get you. What difference does it make? They helped you graduate. You should be happy. Would you rather have failed?"

"That's not the point." I turn off my treadmill, jump on the side rails and turn to face Vick. He's already done the same.

"What is the fucking point?"

"Most people at the company frown upon the idea of rigging a mission like that. The whole thing was a sham. There was no mission, no real target. I killed people for no reason. And they used someone I know as bait to make sure I did the deed. That's bullshit. Would you have wanted to graduate under those terms? I seriously doubt it."

Vick sighs deeply and rubs the sweat from his forehead with a small towel. "Why am I just now hearing about all this? You tell Emily?"

"Yes, I told Emily, but that's because I needed her help escaping. I didn't want to make a fuss until I had more information. Whatever is going on at AWT, it doesn't look good. From what I hear, that place is about to erupt. All because of that last training mission and the implications of it. There's some big secret there that involves Madame K and myself. I'm just trying to figure out what the hell is going on."

"Madame K? Seriously? Jesus, Josey. You sound like a crazy person. Conspiracy theorist much?"

"I know, it sounds bizarre. Believe me, I know. But you have to promise not to tell anyone about this. I need to make one more trip out and then I should have all the information

I need, and hopefully the full truth. It's important to me, Vick."

Vick shakes his head as he looks to the ceiling.

"That's a big ask."

"I know. Just another few weeks or so and I'll reveal everything to you and Emily. Please."

"I'll think about it."

"Fine. I need to take a shower." I jump off the treadmill and start to head out.

"Just one thing," Vick says.

"Yeah."

"A fuckin' cat?" His tone suggests an attempt to lighten the mood.

I chuckle and smile. "Her name is Ginger. And she's cute as hell. Play with her a little bit and she'll have you wrapped around her tiny little kitten paws too."

He playfully grins and shakes his head.

I leave to get cleaned up.

14

Dina arrives at Li Xia's office door a little apprehensive about the conversation she intends to engage in. There are rumblings within the company in regards to leadership, the future, and any fallout that might be on the horizon, should a mutiny occur. The level of distrust from person to person is palpable, every word a riddle, every facial expression a mask. The floor is covered in eggshells and it's getting to the point where the divisions are unclear, potentially leading to a big bang.

As company psychiatrist and counselor, Dina is the pivot point for everyone at AWT, a neutral party for all, despite the fact she's employed by the company itself. They all know it and she does too, but ultimately, she has a job to do and she's beginning to feel unequipped to do it. Every single person she meets with has built a brick wall she is having difficulty traversing. Dina can feel those walls closing in and is beginning to experience the paranoia that others have displayed. She's spent years nurturing, guiding, and evaluating people she believes are good. She sees value in the service the organization provides. She wouldn't be able to do the job otherwise. She frequently sells this point to new recruits at times when there is doubt about the morality of such a place like AWT even existing at all.

For many months, the invisible line each one of them

must draw has been migrating into an area some are uncomfortable standing in. Dina has influence. She often uses rational arguments to steer the ship. It's part of her job, after all, to do so. But now, she's no longer confident she can make a correction and keep the ship from falling off the edge of the world.

Dina knocks twice and hears Li Xia yell, "Come."

Dina enters, closing the door behind her.

"How are you, Dina? Take a seat."

"Been better actually."

"Oh? Do we need to lay you down on a couch and have a go at that psyche?" Li Xia winks.

Dina smiles. "I have a guy for that."

Li Xia nods. "This might be out of line, but does he know exactly what this place is and what you do here?"

"Absolutely. I can't withhold that from him or else our conversations would end up meaningless. He's heavily vetted by the company though."

"So, while you counsel everyone here, he counsels only you?"

"That is correct. I mean, he has other patients beside me, but no one that I'm aware of in this line of work."

"Interesting," Li Xia responds.

Dina pulls a small, silver object from her pocket, presses a button on the top, then places it on Li Xia's desk.

"We have about five minutes before anyone gets suspicious about the silence," Dina says.

The Dean nods.

"Anyway, what did you want to discuss?"

"Let me just preface this conversation by saying I make no judgments either way, so understand that my line of questioning, though it may seem like I'm doubting you, is really just me gathering information in an effort to guide the company into future success."

"When it comes to you, Dina, above everyone here, I always assume that. So, go ahead. Say what's on your mind."

"I've always thought of you as someone that sees

everything. Some months have passed since our latest recruits graduated and moved to the house. I don't know exactly what you know about that last training mission Josey was assigned, the one in Baltimore. I know you prepared it, but I don't know what Madame K may or may not have told you about it."

"Is there a question hiding in all that?"

"Well, yes. That mission was rigged to ensure Josey succeeded. You're aware of that?"

"I am."

"How did you feel about that? Did you and Madame K have a conversation about the implications of doing that?"

"I balked, briefly. She said, 'Not you too.' Her tone made it clear she didn't want to hear any more on the matter. That's where my objection started and ended."

"If you wouldn't mind sharing with me how you really feel, I'd love your insight." Dina makes her best effort to sound agreeable. She needs the people she works with to be completely at ease with her, and not just as a therapist. Having their ears and voices as friends and coworkers is becoming even more important considering the current environment.

"It threw me for a moment. We've never done anything like that around here, not in my time, and I've been around almost since the beginning. After pondering it, I didn't like it one bit." Li Xia has never been one to pull punches. No matter the situation, she is always direct and honest.

"Both Ollie and I agree. We fought it. She threw the hammer down."

"My first thought was, what's so damn special about this woman that she should be given such an assist? Who the hell is this Josey Baldwin? I immediately assumed she and Madame K must have some connection that none of us know about."

"Exactly. It was highly unusual. We give people second chances all the time, but to rig a training mission like that. That blurry line we all operate around suddenly didn't exist and we were deeply troubled by it."

"I don't know if I was deeply troubled, as you say, but it sure as hell didn't fit our normal M.O."

This issue is less catastrophic for Li Xia than for Dina or Ollie, that much is clear. The entire point of this conversation with The Dean was to ascertain her loyalty. The two sides of the coin are obvious. A person is either backing Madame K or they are backing the perceived integrity and hair-splitting morality that has been part of their corporate culture. Many people employed at AWT are only there because they see less gray area in what the company does. A major shift in that area could mean the disenfranchisement of many of AWT's best people, and ultimately, a total collapse. Unless, of course, a change in leadership should come about, one that would restore any lost confidence in the murky good and evil waters that is contract assassination.

As far as Dina and Ollie are concerned, the battle lines have been drawn. On which side do others stand on? The alliances must be known, and for most of the people she has spoken to, the answer is quite obvious. With Li Xia, there is a dichotomy. She respects the authority of Madame K, yet does not support the act. Will she go so far as to firmly oppose Madame K when the time comes?

"I don't know if you've heard the chatter," Dina continues, "but some would say that perhaps the time has come for ... a new direction."

The Dean looks deep into the eyes of Dina, not blinking once as she ponders the idea being presented. She has thought about it before and had come to no clear position. She's never once spoken of it, however, and in this moment, she's not sure she is ready to.

Dina does not break away from the gaze. The bricks of a new wall are assembling themselves as the staring contest ensues. Li Xia is a powerful force at AWT and her allegiance would be an enormous boon to their cause. In her own mind, Dina hears the Dean agree about a leadership takeover. In her stomach, Dina feels the pit of disappointment. Finally, after a full minute, Li Xia breaks the silence.

"I know what you want of me. I just don't know if this one incident is call for that kind of change. Maybe. But maybe not."

"What if there was some connection between Josey and Madame K? How would that shape your opinion?"

"Depends on what that connection is. Do you know something?"

"Ollie has uncovered something interesting. There are still some holes that need to be filled in the story, or so he says. He has yet to reveal the details to me but we should know something soon."

"I'd be very careful digging around in that minefield also known as Madame K's past. You might not like what you find there. I've heard stories. There is no gray area with her, as you would say. Things are very black and white, and they mostly tend to go on the black side."

"We're aware of that. The inherent danger is not lost on us. We just get the sense there is something lurking in that past that could potentially upend everything. It mustn't be swept under the rug. Should it turn out to be nothing of consequence, then we move on."

"Assuming she lets you move on."

"Well, yes. With any luck, she won't find out."

"Oh, Dina. You can't possibly be that naïve. There is a tension in the air around here that every single person has picked up on. It's like trying to see the bottom of the sink through filthy dish water. Most have no idea what it is. Hell, before this conversation I wasn't even truly sure what the stakes were. Now that I do, I kind of wish I didn't."

"What would you have us do? Pretend nothing is wrong?"

"Is there really anything wrong? I'm still not sure that's true. I don't know that putting our lives at risk to find out is worth it. Over some girl that may or may not have any legitimate place here."

"This goes well beyond her presence here and you know it." Dina's voice is growing more intense. "It's about the ideals we stand by and fight for. Innocent lives were lost because of that rigged mission."

"Innocent?" Li Xia interrupts.

"Innocent, yes. We work hard to minimize that, and in that case, we chose to kill people for no other reason than make sure Josey didn't fail the training. That wasn't a real mission. We weren't paid to take out some scumbag."

"Not everyone we kill is a scumbag and you damn well know that. You may be able to push those ones aside in your mind so you can sleep at night, but I don't. I refuse to do this job and pretend it's all roses and rainbows. We kill people, and sometimes those people have done nothing more than be in the wrong place at the wrong time." The Dean rises from her chair. "Maybe it's time for you and Ollie to embrace the truth."

"And what truth is that?"

"That what we do is immoral, no matter how you slice it, and that makes us bad human beings. And we have to be okay with that. In fact, we are okay with it."

Dina puts a finger to her lips in deep thought.

"Our five minutes are up," Li Xia says, then she sits back down.

Dina grabs the device, once again presses the button on the top, and then returns it to her pants pocket. She stands, trying to calm her breathing and heart rate. She respects Li Xia, and inside of her heart and mind, she sees the truth in her words.

"I'm sure we'll talk again soon," Dina says. "I always appreciate your perspective."

The Dean nods as Dina turns and leaves the office.

15

To give myself an extra challenge, I'm taking firearms practice just before dusk. There are many factors that can make this time of day more difficult to get off good shots, and as I've become more efficient in shooting, I feel the need to further advance my skills with these kinds of tests. Mastery in firearms comes with technique and practice. I spend no less than two hours a day, five days a week doing just that.

The first and most obvious difficulty at this hour is the lighting. As the sun sets, the lighting can go from glaring and bright to shadowed and grayish. Shadows, in particular, can play hell with distance judgement. We have all the gadgets of the trade at our disposal, including tiny scopes that actually relay the distance to targets, but just like in grade school where children are taught to do math the long way without the use of calculators, I'm choosing not to use the scopes while training. During a mission, that would be a different story. I use the shit out of them, but there will be occasions when things are not going as expected and I'll have to do without.

The second challenge at twilight is temperature change. As soon as the sun starts to hit the horizon, depending on where a person is in the world and the time of year, there can be a noticeable drop in the temps. Even the slightest shiver in my body, my hands, can throw my aim off several degrees. I often wear layers to make sure that no matter the conditions, I will be prepared.

Today, it's spring and somewhat chilly. The sun setting will drop the temps by ten degrees, rapidly. To test myself, I'm wearing black cargo pants and training boots, but up top, just a white tank undershirt. Even before the sun is fully down, I'm freakin' cold. To get this right, I'll need a little mind-over-matter working for me.

I've setup six targets at varying distances in the field. I'm using a large sniper rifle affixed to a tripod, and that is sitting atop a two-foot tall brick wall. The rifle is a custom job made by AWT. It's pretty damn convenient to have a weapons designer and manufacturer as the front for your contract assassination business. We get all the cool gadgets and toys. They help, but ultimately, our training and skills are the reason we succeed or not. Having great equipment sure makes it nice though. You'll never hear any of us complain.

I fire off a few shots at the closest target, some fifty yards away, just to get a feel for the weapon. This is my first time actually using it. Vick showed it to me a few weeks ago and schooled me in its care and use. I'm getting the nerve to actually try the beast. It feels like I'm launching a cannon.

I grab the tiny pair of binoculars I brought with me and spot the target. Two within the inner circle, two just outside of it on the right. I smile wide. Any of the four would have been kill shots had that target been someone's chest. I'm getting good at this and I'm damn proud of it. My biggest weakness when I entered the Kill Academy has turned into a great asset. I'm nowhere near as proficient as Vick but I'm not far behind.

I advance to the next target, this one is a hundred yards away. At this distance, wind will become a significant factor. We're talking a football field in length. The firing power of this rifle will negate some of that but not all. I look to the trees in the distance. They're swaying from left to right, not constantly, which makes it harder to negotiate. I take careful aim, steady my breathing, discern a pattern in the wind gusts, and just after the trees sway, I fire two shots. My gut tells me I need to adjust more to the left. I repeat my process and once again fire two shots.

I take a look across the field again. The target is that of an average size male. I was aiming for the head. Two of the shots overlapped in the chin area, the other two are somewhere near the left cheek and left ear. I may have over compensated to the left on the third and fourth shots. All four are kill shots, nonetheless. I could have done better but I'm pleased.

"Nice shooting."

I about jump out of my skin and turn around to find Vick standing behind me, munching on a protein bar.

"You fucker. You scared the shit out of me. And yes, my shooting has definitely come a long ways. What are you up to?"

"Had to get outta the house. Emily's all ... PMSing or something."

"Don't be an asshole or I'll punch you in the cock." I stand up and face Vick.

"I'm just saying, she's in a mood. Maybe you could talk to her?"

"Not sure I can help much. There's something going on with her."

"Is it the hack thing? I thought she had that under control."

"I thought so too, but something's up. I assume she's talked to Dina. Apparently, that's not doing any good."

"We can't have her like this all the time. Next mission rolls around, I don't know if I'll feel like I can depend on her."

"Yeah, I know. Damn it. I'll talk to her again, but no promises. If it keeps up, we might have to tell Dina."

"Agreed." Vick looks down at the gun. "If you're done, I'd like to take a crack at that rifle."

"Help yourself. I'll go talk to Emily and chat with you later."

"Thanks."

I find Emily in her room with the door open, sitting on her bed, working away on her laptop. Ginger is napping at the end of the bed.

I knock on the door jamb. "Hey. You busy?"

Emily closes her laptop, places it next to her, and looks to me. "Not really. Come on in."

I walk over to the bed and wake the kitty with a rub to her head. She's disinterested, immediately falling back asleep the second I remove my hand.

"So, let me guess. Vick say something to you?" Emily asks, in no way shocked I'm in here talking to her.

"He did. What happened?"

"It was nothing. He caught me crying a little. He asked me what was wrong. I may have snapped at him. I didn't mean to."

"Emily, we need you to be honest here. Is there something more going on aside from the usual crap?"

Emily covers her mouth with her right hand and looks away.

"Come on. You gotta give us something. I'm just gonna be blunt here. We're beginning to worry about whether we can rely on you for missions. You can trust us. Please tell me what's going on?"

She turns back to me, her eyes watery with tears. "I don't know if I can do this."

"What? The job? You've been doing great."

"I'm really worried," Emily says with tears flowing softly, "worried something bad is gonna happen. Something I won't be able to stop."

"That's ridiculous. I don't know jack-shit compared to you about computer tech, but from my point of view, you're tremendous at this stuff. Just do the best you can. And don't be afraid to get ahold of Marty or Tisha if you need to. They're here to help."

"I just ... have a bad feeling. That's all."

"Is there something specific that's worrying you? You're

kind of starting to freak me out here."

She shakes her head, exhales deeply. "I'm a good person, Josey. I wasn't always in to this hacker game. I got mixed up in some stuff I shouldn't have and I just don't know if I want to do it anymore. But I don't see a way out."

Her tone scares me. I don't know if the guilt of what we do is getting to her or what, but if she doesn't get her head screwed on right, it could mean big trouble on future missions. One mistake from her could endanger all our lives.

"Have you spoken to Dina about your concerns?"

"Not really."

"Well Jesus, Emily! You need to. That's what she's here for. Please. Go talk to her. She might have some insight. Despite my bitching and moaning about our sessions, she does actually help me sort through things from time to time."

"I'm afraid to, to be honest. I don't want them to think I'm weak."

"You're not weak. You're just conflicted. Christ! Now I'm sounding like her." I chuckle.

Emily cracks a smile. "Okay. Don't you guys worry. I'll get it worked out."

"No problem. And don't be afraid to talk to me. I ain't no snitch like Mr. Boy Scout. Our conversations are just between us."

"I appreciate that. Thanks."

"When in doubt, K-I-S-S."

Emily gives me a queer look. "Kiss?"

"Keep it simple stupid. A mentor of mine used to say that to me all the time. I'd always make everything in life too complicated and he'd say 'Keep it simple stupid.'"

Thinking about Mr. Sake has me wishing I could see him again. I don't even know where he is anymore. I lost contact with him a few years ago. For all I know, he could be dead.

"Sounds like a smart man. That's good advice."

"He was. He really was." My mind shifts gears. "I'm going to call up our caretakers and see if they'll deliver us a pizza and some wings. You down?"

"Great idea," Emily says. Her words are filled with sorrow, despite them being agreeable on the surface.

I pet Ginger one more time then leave the two of them alone.

Vick is right to be troubled by Emily's mood lately. If she doesn't figure out what the hell is wrong, and soon, we'd be stupid to keep her on the team. I don't say that lightly. It would be a huge setback for us to lose her. I'm going to work hard to make sure that doesn't happen.

16

"I feel like I can trust you, like we're on the same side here," Ollie says.

"Definitely," Marty responds as they walk along the sidewalk that runs adjacent to the Hudson River. They each took separate cars but ended up in the same place, though twenty minutes apart. Privacy has become a life force of its own in recent months, as valuable as anything. In the world of contract assassination, privacy is always of utmost importance, but around headquarters, every word is a diversion, every smile a cloak. Even the Tech Ops personnel have become embroiled in the mess that is Josey Baldwin.

"There have been some concerning developments in regards to Josey. The picture being developed here is leading us down a path there is no return from."

"I understand. I was just as disturbed by what happened with her as you, so I'm in 'til the end."

"Glad to hear it." They stop several hundred feet from a bridge and turn their attention to the water. There are other people walking and talking, busy with their lives, paying no attention to the two men.

"Care to share these uh ... concerning developments?" Marty asks. He leans sideways onto the rail with his left arm, takes a sip from his paper coffee cup with the other.

"There's still some research left to do before the full story can be told."

"I need to trust you, Ollie. Keeping things from me is not the way to accomplish that."

"I know. There's just more to uncover. I don't want to make assumptions. I need the full truth."

"I understand, but it's hard for me to continually put my life at risk without you giving me something. How about I just ask a few yes or no questions and we'll leave it at that for now?"

Ollie thinks about the idea, rubs his neck, then concedes. "Go ahead."

"At this point, does it appear that Madame K and Josey have a past connection?"

"Yes."

"Would you classify that connection as suspicious or nefarious?"

"Those are two different things. Suspicious, yes. Nefarious, unknown. Last one."

"Are you planning to unseat Madame K should this turn out to be nefarious?"

Ollie pauses. He turns his head away from Marty, searching for his own truth. The obvious answer is yes, but another possibility he has considered is no. Unfortunately, for Ollie at least, answering no means leaving the organization to its own devices and seeking a life somewhere else. Both choices are equally challenging for him. He has always imagined himself as Madame K's successor. He's been groomed for exactly that and he relishes the idea of running AWT in a way he thinks will be better. Though she's hard on him, Ollie sees Madame K as a mentor, a mother-figure, a confidant, and a boss. He can feel those relationships eroding with each passing day, with each development, with each emerging lie.

The flip side is desertion. That could mean death if not done properly. Should he find a way to leave on good terms, Ollie cannot imagine a life outside of AWT. He has enough money to retire to Mexico or South America, something he's dreamt about. But deep inside, he knows he would eventually grow bored of beaches and cocktails. Would he join the private sector and work security? He can't fathom getting up every day for some low six-figures job keeping drunks out of the lobby of a downtown corporate headquarters, or escorting employees out of a building after watching them pack up their desk because they've been fired. He'd rather throw himself off that building then go through that bullshit.

In his heart, he knows the answer, as there isn't really any other choice, not for him. Saying it out loud is the hard part.

Ollie turns to Marty, lets out a deep breath, and looks him square in the eyes. With sincerity and the weight of the words he needs to say pressing hard on his soul, Ollie finally answers with a soft but firm, "Yes." The word wanted to stick to the back of his throat.

Marty nods in support. "I'm with ya, Ollie. Whatever comes to light from all this, we'll deal with it. To reciprocate your trust, I need to share something with you."

"Oh?"

"Yeah. I was going through some traffic and log files on the networks at AWT, something I do from time to time just to make sure everything is moving as it should, when I noticed some unusual activity. This was about a week ago."

"Unusual how?"

"Well, to keep it from being too technical, there were some pings like someone on the outside might be testing the firewall for weaknesses. It piqued my curiosity, so I went back a month, then two, then three, eventually back like six months, and found a pattern of this behavior from various untraceable sources."

"Someone trying to hack AWT's network?"

"Maybe."

"Unsuccessful?"

"As far as I can tell, yes. Now here is where it gets weird. I found a script running that was tracking these pings. A script put in place by someone on the inside. There's really only two people that could have done that, and it wasn't me, so I'll give you one guess to who the other person is."

"Really?"

"Of course, this doesn't mean she's up to no good. She may have noticed the activity too and chose to keep an eye on it. The weird thing is that she didn't tell me about it. Those are the kinds of the things we share with one another. It's protocol."

"Lines are being drawn here. I guess we know what side she's on. Good to know. Do you think that she knows that you know?"

"She doesn't, but I was thinking about confronting her."

Ollie shakes his head.

"Of course not, not now. That was before this conversation. What should I do?"

"Keep an eye on it, just don't get caught. If anything else weird pops up, let me know immediately."

"Sure thing. What are you going to do?"

"I have a few things in play. I should know more soon."

"I just want this shit to be done with. I'm getting an ulcer."

"Soon enough. One way or another."

17

Unknown Location

"I've read through the information you provided, and you were right. With enough time, they will breach the system. The question is, what are they after?"

"At this point, it's impossible to tell. I'm closely monitoring the situation. And speaking of that monitoring, the script I put in place to do it has been noticed. It's only a matter of time before I can no longer hide the truth."

"Just do the best you can. I have a feeling all of this going to come to a head very soon, one way or another. If there are any developments, let me know right away."

"Of course."

"I'm glad I have your trust in this matter. Your allegiance will not be forgotten."

"Thank you. I'm sure we'll be in touch soon."

"Very good."

18

The month of May is here and I couldn't be happier. This spring has been cold, wet, and just chock full of shit I don't want to think about anymore. This morning, the sun is out, more kitty supplies came in, and for at least a short time, all is right with me.

In just a few short weeks, Ginger has nearly doubled in size and is completely box trained. Vick continues to be resistant to her charms but we all know how that goes. The one person in a household that resists the animal becomes that animal's greatest desire. Needless to say, Ginger will not leave him alone. When she is allowed out of my room, she follows him around like a lost puppy. And when Vick thinks no one is around, I catch him petting her and sweet-talking her, and once, despite the fact we are not allowed to take pictures of the house or the property, I snapped a photo on my burner phone of Vick napping on the couch, Ginger curled up happily on his chest. Truth be told, I think I've lost my cat to him. I may feed her and clean the litter box, but Vick and Ginger have become the dynamic duo of this house.

I do admit to a little fleeting boredom which has led me to trying some new fitness stuff, in particular, parkour-style running, jumping, and landing. I've been watching some internet videos on it and sent away for a training kit on Blu-ray. Being strong, fit, and flexible as hell are a few key components to doing it well without injury. My latest attempt at a low-carb diet has helped, giving me higher energy levels. That combined with a more intense strength and conditioning routine has me slimmer and kind of ripped. The mirror version of me is one hot tamale right now.

So far, I've been unsuccessful at recruiting Vick or Emily to join in on the fun. They just watch me sprint from one end of the front porch, and in one smooth movement, hop to the rail, continue flying past it, hit the ground in a roll, and back to my feet running again. They laugh and call me spider monkey. One of these days they're going to be happy I have these new skills and we'll see who's chuckling then. Dickheads.

I'm sitting on the front porch alone, noticing the faux wicker furniture needs hosing off, forcing down an unsweetened coffee with creamer only. Leaving the sugar out of my coffee has probably been the hardest part of going low-carb. That, and bread. And pizza. And donuts. Fuck I'm hungry. That plain yogurt this morning is not cutting it. I need to fry up some bacon or something.

I get up from the chair and turn to head in. Out of the corner of my left eye I see movement coming down the drive. I look out across the lawn and see a black SUV heading toward the house, a nicer one than the guys who bring us stuff. We're not expecting a visit from anyone, so my interest is definitely piqued.

I step to the rail and wait for the vehicle to arrive. It's a company car, one that Dina or Ollie or Madame K would be hauled around in. When it comes to a stop, the rear doors pop open to reveal The Dean and Ollie. This can mean only one thing: mission time.

They walk up to the house, The Dean with a sour look on her face, Ollie carrying a brown accordion-style folder.

"Glad you're here, Josey," The Dean says. I don't like her tone.

"Where else would I be?"

"Oh ... I don't know ... Baltimore?"

Shit. Fuckin' Vick. Little snitch. He'll deny it, of course, but I know he did it. Thankfully, Ollie's here. With any luck, he'll steer this conversation toward leniency.

I take a sip of my coffee. "That is not allowed, Dean."

"She knows," Ollie informs me.

"Damn it! No secrets in this place."

"No, no, let me be clear," Ollie says. "She knows."

"Oh. That kind of know. So, is this one of those, I should go pack my shit kind of situations, or one of those, we good, kind?"

"I want the truth about what happened," the Dean says. "That is the side I'm on. If you sneaking out is the best way for us to find that out, then so be it. When the facts come to light, I will deal with that when the time comes. Until then, I won't interfere."

"How non-committal of you. I don't know if I like that."

"We're on the same side here, Josey," Ollie says. "But time is not. Planning another trip soon?"

"I am."

"Don't get caught. There's a virus of sorts moving swiftly throughout AWT, and if we don't get this figured out soon, the consequences could be dire."

"Roger that." I turn my head in disgust in once again for letting Vick rub off on me with his walkie-talkie speak. I whisper, "Damn it, Vick."

"You okay?" Ollie asks.

"Yeah, it's nothing." I wave it off. "So, where does this leave us? I mean, clearly, we're stepping into some dangerous shit here. How worried should I be?"

"Life and death worried," Ollie says. "All of us. The ramifications ... should this end up going where we think it's going. Best case scenario, there is a peaceful transition of power. Worst case..."

"We're gone-gone?"

Ollie raises his eyebrows and tilts his head.

"Fuck. Nothing can ever be simple for me. I didn't ask for this, you know. Whatever the hell is going on, it's not my doing."

"We know," Ollie responds. "And that's part of why we're here supporting you. Every reasonable person at AWT was against that last mission of yours at the academy. If that's the direction she's taking the company, many of us want no part in it."

"But that's where it gets complicated," the Dean interjects. "This kind of thing has never been done before. I personally don't think it'll go over well, and in this business, maybe we walk away, maybe we don't."

"What if I just walk away now? Forget about what I've found, just walk away from this place and disappear."

"I think we're way past that," Ollie says. "No matter where you go, she'll find you."

"I don't know. I'm pretty sneaky."

"I don't think you have the first clue who you're dealing with," Ollie says.

"I was kidding. I've heard things. I'm taking this seriously. Believe me."

"You damn well better," the Dean snaps. "She'd just as soon put you down as deal with your stupid shit."

"I got it, I got it." I put my hands up in surrender. "You guys didn't drive all the way out here just for this though. So why are you really here?"

Ollie flashes his file folder. "Gather the troops in the war room. Time for another mission."

Our war room, a highly secure and huge part of the basement of the house, is well-lit but quite monotone in it's gray, silvery gray, charcoal gray, and slate gray. It's not meant to be pretty, just functional, and that it is.

The center of the room houses what looks like an eight-foot by five-foot glass table, though it happens to be a giant computer screen where we can display maps and documents – whatever we need. There are four large monitors mounted, two on the north wall, two on the east. Various pieces of computer equipment fill many of the spaces around the room and a large office-grade printer-copier-fax machine sits in the corner. It's quite the impressive setup.

The five of us take places around the center glass screen. Ollie unfurls the papers from his folder, placing them down into three stacks. Vick is at least making eye contact with me again. I know he called and tattled on me, the big baby, but it's Emily I'm really concerned about. I look over to her. She has her head down and she is clearly worried. She hasn't been acting right for a few weeks now and she refuses to divulge the truth of what might be troubling her. Perhaps the attempted hacking of our house network has her bothered, perhaps it's something else. I wish she'd open up to me the way I have with her. The last thing this team needs is for her to crack open like a busted watermelon, especially as we're about to embark on a new mission. At some point, I'm going to have to try and talk to her again, see if I can't make some progress.

"Okay team, we got a mission here," Ollie says. "This one's a doozy and probably going to be your most difficult one yet. It will require each one of you to be at your best, so harness all those lessons, all that training, and use it well."

"With that windup, I don't know whether to be excited or scared," I say.

"Be cautious ... and be smart. That is what you need to be," the Dean says.

"To be successful, each of you will play a significant role on this one, including the Secondary Point." Ollie looks straight at me. "Josey, you'll be Secondary this time around. Vick, you're Point, obviously."

"Good," Vick says as he rubs his hands together, anxious to get started. "What do we have?"

Ollie slides the first stack of papers over to Vick. I'm standing right next to him so I read along. The mission will be the most complicated one we've had to date.

There are two hard targets. The main one is a Gus Taggert, Texas oilman worth several hundred million dollars. That will make him difficult to get at. Guys like him have lots of enemies, palatial estates, highly secured office buildings, and sometimes, even bodyguards that usually double as their drivers. And in Texas, he'll no doubt be packing heat himself and probably be a damn good shot.

The second unlucky bastard we have to take out is Denis Koplen. He is the unofficial righthand man of Mr. Taggert. The two can be seen together at all hours of the day, in any number of capacities, however, Denis is not actually employed by Mr. Taggert. Their relationship, as it turns out, goes deep down the rabbit hole of deplorable behavior. Denis gets his money from an underground sex trafficking ring that he facilitates for the rich sumbitches of Texas.

Nestor and Sofia Kokinos, brother and sister, are the ones paying for this contract. They come from a wealthy Greek family and are looking for a little justice, and I'm sure a shit-ton of revenge for their sister, Phoebe, who lost her life in that sex trafficking racket. Apparently, Mr. Taggert and Mr. Koplen have no obvious connection to the sex trafficking and have been untouchable from a legal standpoint. That's where the Kill Team comes in. This kind of case, at least for me, makes the job easier. If I'm to be completely honest, my blood is boiling as I read the dossier. I love the idea of putting an end to these assholes and their sex trafficking ring. I've always stood up for the little guy, the disadvantaged, the innocent woman being mishandled by men. I only wish I was working Point on this one. I'm sure as hell going to be hands on, as much as Vick will allow. He's in charge and I do have to respect that.

To date, all my work for AWT, at the academy and as a Kill Team member, has taken place in the northeastern part of the country. This one will take us to Houston, Texas, and possibly across the border and into Mexico. The underage sex ring operates mostly out of Houston and Galveston, though all signs point to a rendezvous place setup just across the border or in rural Texas. When Ollie hinted to the difficulty of this mission, he was not fucking around. We'll have months of preparation, recon, living away from home, and travel across the border.

I only wish Emily had her head on straight right now. She could end up being a liability if she's moody, crying all the time, downtrodden to the point of being useless. What I can't really figure out is at what point we talk to The Dean or Dina about Emily? I don't want to jump the gun here but I also want Emily to have a chance to figure this out on her own. Luckily, we'll have quite a stretch of time to get this one done.

"So, any questions?" the Dean asks.

"I see here in the file it says minimal casualties, but that's always the case. Why mention it like this?" Vick asks.

"The Kokinos see only fault in the two targets, not their staff, their henchmen, their families," Ollie says. "They would prefer a non-lethal method of dealing with anyone else unless absolutely necessary."

"And what that means," the Dean interjects, "is that you'll need to hide your identities during the actual kill, masking your faces in some way. And taking out the targets should be done in locations of isolation to avoid witnesses. Consider this priority number one."

"They don't want this looking like a Mexican drug cartel massacre," Ollie says. "Two dead, and they want the world to know those two alone were the targets. Like a karma thing. They want the sex trafficking blown wide open, with fingers pointed right at Taggert and Koplen."

"How do they plan to keep their own hands clean in all this?" I ask.

"Other than us, no one else will know about the Kokinos involvement," Ollie answers. "Their sibling was never positively identified as a victim of the sex trafficking. It cannot be traced back to them."

I glance over to see how Emily is handling all this information. She's taking shallowed and labored breaths.

"Emily, you okay?" I ask.

"Actually, I'm not feeling well. Nauseous. I think I need to go to the bathroom. Excuse me."

Emily runs out of the room and up the stairs.

"She going to be alright?" the Dean asks.

"Oh yeah, a little food poisoning or something," I say "She wasn't feeling good earlier. I'm sure she'll be fine." I have no idea what's actual wrong with her. Just throwing up a little smoke screen for my team member. I hope to hell it has nothing to do with her recent worries. If it does ... shit, shit, shit.

Vick raises an eyebrow that only I can see. I give him a subtle wave of my hand to signal it was no big deal. He shrugs it off.

"Well, for Emily's part, she'll have her work cut out for her," Ollie says. "The office building of Mr. Taggert is highly secured with cameras everywhere. His home is no less burdensome from that perspective."

"She can handle it," I say. "We trust her completely." I may be overselling it little, but for now, I don't want the uppers getting even a whiff of doubt about her. Not yet.

"Study up," the Dean says. "We want you guys ready to head down there in two to three weeks. Check in with us if you have any questions. And don't be afraid to lean on Marty or Tisha if the tech stuff gets too crazy. Okay?"

Vick and I both nod and continue flipping through all the paperwork as we stand there.

I look over and see Ollie suggest to the Dean with his eyes that he wants her to leave. She nods.

"Hey, Vick," the Dean says, "Greg was telling me about that new rifle he had sent over. Care to show it to me before I leave. Been curious to see it."

"Oh, hell yeah," Vick says. "That thing is sweet. Follow me. I have it in a case in the dining room."

"Perfect. After you."

They head off and once out of earshot, Ollie starts.

"You don't have much time. If you're going to check out Allister Coal, I'd do it soon. I get the feeling at headquarters that every step we take, someone is two steps ahead."

"Well, that's not good."

"No, no it isn't. I can feel the walls closing in, and if we don't take control of the situation soon, all hell is going to break loose."

"Are we, in like, real danger here? Do you think she'd actually do something?"

"Let me be clear so there's no doubt. Madame K is a dangerous woman with motives none of us quite understand. If a mutiny at AWT is on the horizon, not all of us are going to leave with our heads intact. I'd like to keep mine. I'd like you to keep yours too. None of this shit is your fault."

I gulp hard and rub the sides of my neck with both hands. "I like my head."

"Well, let's try to keep it attached then."

"I know one thing, now that we have a mission, getting to Pennsylvania seems impossible."

"I figured as much. I guess it's just going to have to wait."

"Once the mission is done, I'll get over there as quickly as I can."

"Good. Be extra careful. Two steps ahead, remember."

"I will. It's cute that you're so concerned. It's kinda hot, actually."

Ollie gives me a super-serious stare.

"I'm just saying. Before you leave, can I ask you something? Did Vick tattle on me for leaving the house?"

"Of course. Be careful around him. He's a helluva partner to have, but he definitely has an affinity for the rules of the game. Before you leave again, tell him what's going on. If he calls headquarters again and talks to the wrong person, game over."

"I've already started the big reveal to him. I'll finish up before I go."

"Good. Let's head up and check out this sweet rifle."

I smile. I'm growing terribly fond of Ollie, in a way that is kind of scaring me. When I first met him, he couldn't have been more standoffish and unlikable, but now that I've cracked him open like a big sexy piñata, I can see the real Ollie. He's a good man with his heart in the right place and

105

I'm glad he's on my side.

19

Madame K's office at AWT

In a recent remodel, Madame K had her office moved from the northeastern top floor corner office to a freshly constructed and much larger space centered on the north wall, with a spectacular view of the street and the nearby buildings. She situated her desk in front of the northern wall of windows, her back to it, so she could easily spin around and catch a view anytime she wished. There are now four comfy black leather club chairs on the guest side of the desk instead of the original two.

The east wall has a high-quality reproduction of HR Giger's 'Birth Machine', some five feet tall and over three feet wide. The image of a traverse cut pistol with bullets in the form of bizarre humanoids fits perfectly in the office of the CEO and President of a company like AWT, a company that gives birth to professional assassins and manufactures the weapons they will use to destroy the misshapen citizens of a world that longs for some type of relief from the chaos.

There are three doors in the room – an entry door, a door to the bathroom, and one to a small closet where Madame K keeps a selection of clothing and shoes so she can change quickly for any occasion without having to go home.

She sits quietly, the windows at her back as she reads The

Wall Street Journal and sips a fresh cup of cinnamon orange tea. As calm as she seems, in truth, she is toiling with uncertainties, many beyond her control. And despite being in charge, her own hubris requires she at least attempt to navigate the complicated circumstances wafting around the company. That starts with her second in command, Ollie.

Through the phone intercom, "Madame K, Ollie is here."

Madame K presses the SEND button on her desk phone and says, "Send him in."

Ollie turns the metal handle and pushes open the heavy wooden door. He steps into the room, the door closing automatically with a whiff and a click.

"Come sit," Madame K says. She carefully folds her newspaper and places it on the edge of her desk.

"Thank you." He takes the seat left of center. "I tell ya, every time I come in here, that view gets me."

"It sure does help me feel like I'm not locked up inside all day."

"I bet. So, what'd you need?"

"As you know, we've been working on a deal to supply weapons and equipment to J & R Security out of Salt Lake City, but they need a little hand-holding, I think, to get the deal done."

"Okay. So, when are you leaving?"

"Actually, I'm sending you. I think Roy will respond better to your particular brand of machismo, if you know what I mean."

Internally, Ollie is already resisting. As far as he knows, the deal is going well and he doubts he could personally make anything better. He smells bullshit.

"I'm confused. I thought that deal was pretty well locked in. Be kind of overkill at this point."

"Let's just call it a gut feeling. I'd like someone there to represent us, other than the fucking lawyers, just in case they have any last-minute doubts."

"Certainly, there's someone else you could send. I mean, we just gave the team a new mission and I'd really like to be around when they get started."

"Oh, nonsense. Li Xia can handle all that. I need you there. You leave in two weeks. I've already arranged your travel."

Ollie struggles to find another excuse not to go but comes up empty. His face cannot hide his displeasure. Madame K could care less. He gets a sense that she is trying to get rid of him for a time. He wonders what might happen while he's away and what he might be coming back to, if he comes back at all.

Playful in tone to hide the seriousness of the question, Ollie asks, "Why do I get the feeling you're trying to get rid of me?"

Madame K looks Ollie straight in the eyes, takes a sip of her tea, then plainly states, "I expect regular updates from Utah. Thanks for coming in."

"Well, I better go pack." Ollie stands and walks out of the office without another word.

As the door shuts behind him, Madame K turns to her massive windows and smiles with a wicked grin. For both of them, the game has escalated.

20

I need this mission right now, more than I can say. Emily is on edge. Vick is barely speaking to me. I'm wearing my own despair like a curled up shingled roof in need of replacement. Things seem to be falling apart in the house right now and the only thing I think can fix it is work. If we can shift our focus to the job and away from the inside of our own heads, we'd all be better off. So, I need this mission. We ALL need this mission.

We've been at it for about ten days now, just laying the groundwork for our Texas mission. There isn't much we can do until we actually get there but a little prep work can go a long way. I've been studying maps of the area, the good parts of town, the bad ones, the freeways, traffic patterns, weather norms – real nerdy stuff.

Vick is doing some of the same but he's also spending time carefully selecting the weapons to take. He even went to HQ for a two-day intensive recon training exercise with Nazar, just to make sure his game is up. I have to admire his dedication.

Emily's been doing what Emily always does – saving blueprints, maps, gathering data about traffic, weather, and crime, much like I have. For her part, however, she is making sure there are ways to access all that information without an internet connection. If we need a map and the wi-fi or the 4G goes down, we'd be fucked. Can't have that.

At this point, we're close to leaving for Texas, but there's one big thing the team has left to decide before we do. I've called a meeting in the dining room to work out the details.

At the table, Vick sits at the far end closest to the kitchen. Emily and I are across from one another.

"What is so fucking mission critical that you have us sitting here like we're about to have a family meeting?" Vick asks. He's angry and I'm beginning to worry his attitude might compromise the mission, although, I'm not sure he's truly mad. One thing I've noticed about Vick is that he gets angry when he's anxious or nervous. We're going to have a talk about all this before we leave. If this shit hovers while the mission is ongoing, we'll all end up dead. I'm not terribly interested in that.

"Well, brother Vick, there's one last detail we need to work out before we leave."

"Get on with it," Vick says.

"Codenames. We need codenames for the mission."

Vick lowers and tilts his head, locks eyes with me.

"Come on," I plea. "We gotta do it. So, let's. Right now."

Emily sighs. Vick shakes his head.

"Can't you guys feel it?"

"Feel what?" Emily asks.

"The figurative bomb that's about to go off in this house." I said figurative because in our line of work, you can't always count on those kinds of metaphors not to be taken literally. I didn't want Emily and Vick diving under the table.

They look to one another, then look back to me.

"I mean, Jesus. Between your," I point to Emily, "moping around here, distant and crying ... and your," I glance over to Vick, "incredible green monster routine and not speaking to anyone, I'd say the roof is about to blow off this place. That doesn't even include the shit I'm dealing with, which is turning out to be one big cluster fuck. But hey," I throw my hands up, "I'm sucking it up, doing my job, and trying damn hard to trust you two and not fuck this up. What's your excuses?'"

"It's real hard to trust you too, especially when you're keeping some big secret that could affect all of us," Vick says. "How about that?"

"He's got a point, Josey," Emily says.

"Look, this thing I'm digging into is touchy and it involves the company, in a BIG way, and if I tell the wrong person what I'm up to, it could get me killed. Plain and simple. And Vick, don't pretend like you didn't already play tattle-tale about my little excursion. I know you called Ollie."

Emily throws a look of disgust and shock at Vick.

"You broke the rules!" Vick snaps. "You put all of our lives in danger by pulling that crap. What was I supposed to do?"

"You could be a little more understanding," I say. I place both my hands on my head, simulate pulling my hair out, and let out a little growl. I close my eyes and try to center myself. I need to steer this conversation to a resolution. They can both sense it too.

"Sounds like we need a reboot, guys," Emily suggests. "What can we do to get past this?"

Vick seems frustrated but his face softens as I'm sure he thinks more about the implications of not fixing this. "Suggestions?" Vick asks.

"All of us have shit to deal with, personal shit, but in this house, in this job, we have to come together or we're going to end up dead. That's the bottom line." I pause to gauge reactions. Emily and Vick are lightly nodding.

"This mission is going to test us, each in different ways, but more importantly, it's going to test us as a team," I continue. "For now, we need to leave everything else behind and focus one hundred percent on the mission. When it's done, we can take a night to get everything out in the open between us, and when the dust settles, we'll see where we're at, for good or bad."

Emily throws her head back, eyes closed. She lets out a heavy and troubled breath.

"I think I can do that," Vick says. "But we each have to promise full transparency from that point on, or I don't know if I can continue on here." He's dead serious.

"I can do that," I say, and I believe it.

Emily takes a few more deep breaths before lowering her head and opening her eyes.

"Okay," Emily squeaks out. Her response is less convincing than I'd like but considering the stress she's been under, I'll take it.

"Great. This is good. We can do this, guys. We need to." I have never considered myself the motivational speaker type but my efforts seem to have worked. I can feel some of the tension leave the room. Hopefully we can keep this trust-monster chained up until we get back from Texas.

Vick starts to rise from his chair.

"Hang on, hang on," I say, ushering him back into his seat with my hand. "We do actually still need to pick our codenames, so go. Start throwing out some ideas."

Both of them appear disinterested.

"Come oooooon," I plea. "Let's have some fun with it."

"Huey, Louie, and Dewey," Vick blurts with little enthusiasm.

"You're a quack," I say.

Emily snickers and shakes her head. "I suppose there's no ducking this discussion."

Emily and I both bust out laughing. "Fowl! Now that's the ticket," I say.

Vick forces a smile. "You two are such dorks."

"Birds of a feather," Emily says.

"Oh shit, we're on fire," I say. Steering the conversation, "Not the ducks. What else we got?"

"Moe, Larry, and Curly," Vick says.

"Too old school for me," Emily says.

"Oh, oh, oh, I got it. What about Rock, Paper, Scissors?" I ask.

"Hmmm," Vick says. "I think I like it."

"Yeah, I like it too," Emily adds. "Rock, paper, scissors.

That's a good one. So, who's who?"

"Well, clearly Vick is the Rock," I say.

"Ummm, yeah," Vick responds. "And I'd say you're clearly the scissors. If one of us is going to stab somebody, it'd be you."

We all share in a giggle. This conversation is a great way for us all to loosen up and begin trusting one another again. And it couldn't have happened at a better time.

"I guess I'm paper then. Which really makes too much sense when you think about."

"Yes!" I yelp.

"Say it, don't spray it," Vick says. "You got spittle on my face, you disgusting animal."

"Sorry," I say. "But let's be real," I stop and simulate jerking off with my right hand. "That's not the most disgusting thing you've gotten on your face."

Vick and Emily share in their best faces of shock and repulsion.

"You two are such fucking prudes," I say. "I think our next mission needs to be us going out and getting you two laid. Seriously."

"Don't be a snot," Emily retorts. "I've never had any trouble finding gentlemen callers. It's just a little difficult being trapped inside this house."

"Gentlemen callers?" I playfully sneer. "Who talks like that?" I laugh. Vick joins in.

"You two are such buttheads," Emily says, joining in on the laugh. "So, are we good here? I mean, I need to get back to work. We'll be leaving in a few days."

"I suppose so," I answer. "Vick?"

"We're done."

We all leave the table and separate to our rooms.

I sit in bed, pleased with the evening's conversation, hopeful we've managed to bench the built-up tension. This big mission, I have a feeling, is going to make or break us as a Kill Team. We'll either come back stronger than ever or ready

114

to crack. For the sake of us all, I hope it's the former. And this, of course, assumes that everything with Madame K and AWT pans out on the good side of things. I need to make a trip to Pennsylvania but I just don't think I'm going to have time to deal with that before we head to Texas. One thing at time.

After sitting alone for ten minutes, there's a knock at my door.

"Come."

Vick opens the door and enters, closing the door behind him. He steps to the end of the bed.

"What's up?"

I see Vick's expression go from neutral to serious in the blink of an eye.

"I need to tell you something, out of respect for our attempts at trust building."

"Okay."

"With all this talk about your last test mission being rigged, it got me thinking about the one we're about to go on."

"Oh yeah? In what way?" I don't know if I want to hear what he's about to say.

"I've never told you this, but I worked for the F.B.I. for a short time before coming here."

"Honestly, that doesn't surprise me."

"Yeah, well, it's not easy for me to admit, but I had to leave the F.B.I. because I kind of fell apart after my last assignment."

"Really? Wow. What happened?"

"I, uhhh, there was a fire and two people died. I got panicked and jumped the gun. I broke protocol and entered a building before the rest of my team arrived. I didn't know it was rigged to explode. How could I? I was thrown back like twenty feet.

"The guys we were there to arrest found out we were coming, somehow, and they had already bailed, leaving behind two people and explosives."

"I'm really sorry, Vick. Truly. So, how is this connected to my fake mission? I don't get it."

"That assignment was on the border of Texas and Mexico and it was to break up a sex trafficking ring."

I'm stunned by this development. Is this déjà vu all over again? I feel my stomach drop.

"Now, before you get any ideas, I don't think the game is fixed here. That's not why I'm telling you all this."

"You know how I feel about coincidences."

"Me too, but I don't think there's any connection, I just wanted you to know this one hits close to home for me. None of the names of the people involved in our mission are familiar to me, at all. We got word of a location close to Mexico that might have been used as a transitional spot for getting girls across the border. I got there first, thought I heard screaming, entered the building. BOOM!"

"Jesus, Vick. That's just crazy. And nothing about this seems familiar or even gives you the slightest feeling of doubt?"

"Well, yeah, it seems familiar, but I'm pretty sure it's only because of the location and the sex trafficking, not because the details line up to me. We never even found out who was behind the trafficking, and worse yet, the two bodies found inside were never positively identified. I don't see any way this could possibly be connected to me."

I'm dumbfounded by this information and can hardly see straight. The words of Emily come to mind. She recently shared with us that she had a bad feeling about this mission. This info does nothing to quell that for me. How would she know anyway? She wouldn't. Her own anxiety is just a coincidence. And there's that word again. Coincidence.

"Have you told Ollie?"

"No way. They know the details of my time at the F.B.I. If they suspected something, there's no way in hell they would've handed this mission over to us. Right?"

I tilt my head with insecurity. "I'd like to think so, but with the shit I've been dealing with, I don't know what to believe anymore. You tell Emily?"

"God no. I want to, but she's stressed out enough. She might just crack if I tell her."

"That's a good point. I hate to keep something like this from her though. I guess we have to ask ourselves, is there a greater risk in telling her or a greater risk in keeping it from her, just from a mission standpoint?"

"Like I said, she might just crack."

"True. She won't be on location, or at least not too close to the action, so if anything goes down, she should be safe. We'll just have to be careful. Full disclosure, if shit goes down, you're taking the fall and I'm just gonna sneak out and go home." I smile.

"That's fair. At least I'm Point."

"Oh, Vick. Vick, Vick, Vick. You sure about all this?"

He nods. "Sure as I can be."

"I guess that's just gonna have to do."

21

A cell phone comes to life with a vibration. The hacker answers, uncertainty pulsing through their fingers as they swipe the screen.

"Yes?"

"Our side is clear. How does it look on your end?"

"Complicated." The hacker sighs.

"Will there be any issues? I sense doubt in your voice."

"No issues."

"Just think about Millie and Frank whenever you're feeling overwhelmed. If all goes well, you'll be home free."

"I don't need reminded. It will get done. Is that all?"

"Don't fuck this up."

The line goes dead. The hacker wants desperately to toss the phone across the room but holds back.

For nearly a year, the preparations for an upcoming moment will bring everything to a head. Failure will not be tolerated.

22

Houston – Thirty-four days later
Wednesday

I was told it might be uncomfortably hot on this mission. I underplayed the warning. We've been in the Houston area for three weeks doing reconnaissance and I've spent damn near the entire time sweating it out. Whenever possible, I wear a tank-top, but that is rarely practical when I'm sneaking around, scouting locations, trying to stay invisible. I brought two, thick black hoodies with me. After just ten days in the Lone Star State, I had to go out and buy five more. I did find thinner ones, not much thicker than a t-shirt, but still. I'm going through one per day at this point, fully saturating them during a given twenty-four-hour period. To keep from doing laundry every two days, my wardrobe needed supplementation.

Thank the assassination gods I was already in great shape when this mission arrived, or I'd probably have heatstroke by now. When out and about, Vick and I have both decided that no fewer than two one-liter bottles of water would be carried by us at all times. With temps in the low nineties on most days and high humidity, we can't be too careful. Even at the end of day, after a nice, cool shower, it takes forever to dry off.

After nearly a month here, we're well on our way. For security's sake, we're staying at three different cash-only motels, all under assumed identities. We only know our own fakes names too, in case we are infiltrated by an outside party. This will make it harder to track us all down. Say hello to Mandy Downing. My friends call me Scissors.

We drove all the way down to Texas in a white van that will act as our team headquarters. For the most part, the van will be the only place we are ever together, at least until near the end of the mission. The vehicle has hidden caches of weapons, a stash of high-tech devices like dummy phones, laptops, binoculars, and a bunch of other stuff Emily can use to blackout or subvert technology and networks. I know we're all excited to put some of this expensive crap to use.

At the moment, there is plenty of piddly shit for each of us to do, all in the name of recon and preparation. For my part as Secondary Point, Vick has assigned me to scout the comings and goings of Denis Koplen, specifically when he is not with Mr. Taggert. Their interactions are frequent but not every day. Once I tracked him down, I've had no trouble trailing him.

I found a small Ford pickup truck for sale on Craigslist. Digging deep to find the charming version of myself, I got the guy down to eight hundred bucks. Mandy, when she wants to, has a great smile and a highly flirtatious nature. Her evil twin, Josey, will shoot you in the face if the money is right.

After two and a half weeks of following Denis around, I have discovered, that like most of us, he is a man of routine. Around 8:45 am, he leaves his high-rise apartment building, one of those kind that has luxury apartments, twenty-four-hour security, a pool on the roof, and an underground parking garage.

He drives a black late model, Mercedes S-class, a vehicle that costs more than every car I have ever owned, combined. And like most Houstonians, he drives like a bat out of hell with little regard for public safety. He has me wishing I had bought a sports car instead of the bucket of crap I did. I've almost been in four car accidents trying to keep up with him.

He stops every day at a local diner, a real mom and pop kind of place, and drinks three cups of black coffee with his Denver omelet, hash browns, and whole wheat toast. He eats alone, reads the paper, not once checking his phone. When he's done, he leaves a twenty-dollar bill on the table with the check and spends ten minutes in the bathroom.

Once in his car and before pulling away from the restaurant, Denis makes a few phone calls. I have a special listening device and have been able on occasion to get close enough to hear him speak to Mr. Taggert.

In fact, I sit here today in my rust bucket, windows down and already sweating, parked just three cars away from Denis, listening. It's Wednesday, so most likely after his breakfast, he'll head to his bank on West Lafayette, after which he'll disappear into a non-descript office building for four hours. We tried to figure out exactly what business was being held in that location, but to date, Emily has turned up the name of an LLC, Bowerstone, Inc., and nothing else. The company is listed as a consulting firm, but shit, that could mean anything. Our guess is that it's some kind of front for laundering money or other illegal activities.

Denis finally places the phone call. I can't hear the person on the other end, but I can hear Mr. Koplen just fine.

"Mr. Taggert."

...

"I'm doing well, thank you."

...

"I just wanted to make sure our July eighteenth dinner meeting to discuss the Jackson house thing was still a go?"

...

"Yes. I have the backroom at Dawson's reserved for us."

...

"It won't be a problem. I'll make sure we're covered."

...

"Friday for drinks?"

...

"See you then. Bye."

Holy shit! I need to talk to Emily and Vick about this. We have a potential date and location where both of our targets will be present and alone. That could be our opportunity. I decide to end my stakeout for the day. Denis pulls away from the parking lot. I'm almost jumping out of my skin with excitement for this possible breakthrough.

Dawson's? I need to look that up. I grab my phone from the cup holder, swipe the screen, and bring up the internet. I type in: Dawson's Houston. It's a steakhouse, southeast on the way to Galveston. And what's the Jackson house thing? We've long suspected they have a place just across the border where the sex ring clients go to buy and use girls. If that's the case, that might be an even better place for us to do our jobs. We can simultaneously take down their business and fulfill our contract. I know Vick won't find that first part a necessary part of the equation, or one we should even be thinking about, but it is to me. Even if I have to handle it alone, I will.

I text Emily and Vick and ask for a van meeting this evening. Emily is the one in charge of the van and it's her mode of transportation. We agree to meet in the abandoned parking lot of old K-Mart on the southwest side of Houston.

I put my phone away, and just as I'm about to start the truck, I feel the intimately familiar sting of a knife blade tip in the side of my neck. I close my eyes for three seconds and try to catch my breath. Goddamn it, Josey!

"Don't you fuckin' move or I'll slice you up." The man's voice is unknown to me. Could be a random attempt at robbery. He clearly has no idea who he's trying to jack.

"I wouldn't do anything stupid if I were you," I say.

"Shut up! I know who you are and I have a message for you. Drop the investigation."

"I don't know what the hell..." I stop as he presses the

knife just a little deeper into my skin, not quite breaking the surface, but close.

"I said shut up. If it's discovered you're digging around again, there'll be consequences. We're watching."

I feel the knife twist ever so slightly then release. Blood trickles from the wound.

"Look, I don't know who you are or what you want, but I'm no one to be trifled with."

I wait for a response. Silence. I count to five then dare to turn around. Shit. The guy is gone. I throw the door of the truck open and jump out, surveying the area in all directions. There are people coming and going everywhere but no one stands out. That'll teach me not to keep an eye on my blind spots.

I wet my fingertips with my tongue and wipe the blood from my neck, then wipe my fingers on the right sleeve of my hoodie. With this threat to my investigation into my past and the knife at my neck, I'm instantly reminded of something that happened a long time ago, something I will never forgot.

Fifteen years ago

The party had been raging most of the evening. My room in the tiny house was barely ten feet removed from the living room where the adults were up drinking and smoking and carrying on. I couldn't sleep. I had no idea what the occasion was, I only remember two men and three women coming over after dinner with a twenty-four pack of canned beer and several duffel bags of who knows what.

I went to my room early that night by instruction from Jack, my foster father. He and his wife Marcy had taken me in for a brief stint when I was ten years old. That night, I huddled in my room with the family dog, Roscoe, reading through magazines and watching TV while the adults partied hard. Thankfully, it was a Saturday night and I didn't have to get up for school the next day. No one would sleep that night, at least not until after the cops showed up.

At some point after two a.m., one of Jack and Marcy's friends, Quentin, I think his name was, came into my room and proceeded to yell at Roscoe. The dog barked whenever anyone from the living room got too loud, like yelling loud. With those drunk assholes, it was about every three minutes.

"Shut the duck up, you stupid fog!" he ordered. He laughed hysterically at his word jumble. When he finally noticed me sitting on the bed, he became oddly curious. He cocked his head and just stared at me for what seemed like five minutes, although, it was more like twenty seconds.

"Get outta my room. He ain't hurting nobody," I barked.

Quentin turned his head back out the door and yelled, "This kid of yours has a mouth on her."

From the living room, Jack hollered back, "She ain't our kid. We're doing a favor for someone. I told you that, dumbass."

Quentin turned back to me. From his pocket he slid a knife, switchblade style.

"You ever see one of these?" He pressed the button, the blade springing forth with a snap.

Roscoe sat on the floor at the end of my bed. He growled.

I couldn't understand why he brought out the knife. Was he being threatening or just showing it off? I remember feeling scared.

"Marcy!" I yelled.

Roscoe barked twice.

"Shut up, dog!" Quentin said. "I will kick the shit out of you."

"You will not," I said. I jumped from the bed, stepped in front of Roscoe, and ushered him behind me. Roscoe was the only thing in the Paar household I cared about. There was no way in hell I was going to let some drunk asshole hurt him. "Get out of my room."

"I'm your elder, you snot. You don't ... tell me what to do."

From the living room, "Quentin, get outta there!" Jack said.

Before I could evade, Quentin grabbed me by the arm and twisted me around, pulling me near. In a matter of seconds, he had the tip of the knife to my throat.

"You need to learn some respect, little girl."

"Let go of me," I said, squirming with no luck.

I could feel the tip of the blade ever so slightly pierce my skin, a tiny trickle of blood running down my neck.

"Stop moving around." He knew what he had done and tried to blame it on me. "Now look what you did."

I put a finger to my neck and the blood streak. When I pulled my hand away and saw the red on my finger, I let out a scream so high-pitched it could've curdled milk.

"What the fuck happened?" Jack said, suddenly present at the door to my room.

Quentin whipped us around to face Jack.

Marcy and a few of the others soon appeared behind Jack.

When Jack saw the blood, he about snapped. His eyes went wide and crazy. He rushed Quentin, smacked the knife from his hand, and grabbed him by the throat with both hands.

Marcy snuck around them and took me by the hand, guiding me and Roscoe from the room. It wasn't long before a small melee ensued between four or five of them as they tried to keep Jack from tearing Quentin apart.

On our way to the kitchen to get my neck cleaned up, Marcy noticed the flashing blue and red of police cruiser lights from around the living room curtains, then there was a pounding on the front door that made all of us jump out of our skins.

Marcy yelled, "Just a minute!"

There was a mad scramble by Marcy and two of the other women to clean up the drugs and associated paraphernalia.

Another pounding on the front door. "Baltimore Police Department. Please open the door."

"Just one minute," Marcy answered as she arm-swept several items off the coffee table into a duffel bag. She zipped the bag and then tossed it to one of the other women, pointing to the back bedroom. Marcy remembered me suddenly. "Go to the kitchen, Josey. I'll be there in a second to clean you up. Go."

I did as instructed. I took a kitchen towel, ran water over the end of it, and wiped the blood from my neck. The wound was small, maybe the size of the tip of a ballpoint pen. It had already stopped bleeding. I found a napkin and held it to my neck just to be sure.

When the cops finally came in, they had to break up the still ongoing fight in my room. In their drunken states, one of them let slip what really caused the fight: Quentin had put a blade to my throat. The officer inspected my neck and swiftly removed me from the home. Eventually, they got a hold of Dr. Greenberg, and that was that. I never saw the Paars or Roscoe again.

To be awoken in the early hours of a Sunday to deal with me did not sit well with Rosemary. I told her exactly what happened, and as I should have expected, she turned the entire incident into something I caused and could have easily prevented. She made it clear there would no future foster excursions for me, and any chance of adoption was all but gone.

I was always told that my age made it difficult, if not impossible, for me to be adopted or even get into foster care. I'm beginning to think that was all a ruse. As I think back, I can recall plenty of times when other kids my age and even older would get adopted or go into long-term foster care, yet I was always passed by – no meet and greets, no interviews.

A good children's home is more like a bus station, with the children coming and going frequently, only a few staying for any period of time. The ones that get left behind are often the most troubled kids of all, the ones that come from seriously abusive situations, drug houses, you name it. The system makes every effort to find guardians and adopters but not all kids can manage a successful transition, and I was no exception.

A few weeks before that night with Quentin and the knife, I was brought to Rosemary's office at the end of a late February day. I sat outside her door for a few minutes before they knew I was there, eavesdropping on the conversation. I couldn't hear every detail but the gist of it involved doing Rosemary a favor, a temporary situation, something about money.

Rosemary came out to get me, a little surprised to see me sitting there, no doubt wondering how much I may have heard, though she didn't ask. I followed her in, taking a seat in a side chair on the left wall. She returned to her desk chair.

To my shock, a man and woman I had never seen before were sitting in front of the desk. I remember being instantly nervous and excited. That moment was exactly what I had always imagined it would be like to meet the people that would become my adopted family. The funny thing was the energy in the room - not at all what I expected. I figured they would feel about the same way I did, but as best as I could tell, they didn't want to be there. Plus, it was late, like seven p.m., which was highly unusual for any meeting at that place.

"Josey, this is Jack and Marcy Paar," Rosemary said.

I smiled nervously. I remember them looking over to me and offering up slight head nods.

"They've volunteered to take you in for a while. Nothing permanent, just an opportunity to give you a little break from this place. How does that sound?"

"Really?" I said. "That would be awesome."

Looking back now, that break was really for her. I was a handful, even at ten years old, and I'm sure she was at her wit's end. In my naivety, I gladly went along.

"Do you have kids?" I blurted.

"We don't," Marcy answered. She had an accent, southern, but not deep south. She wasn't from Baltimore, I knew that. "But you'll have your own room. And you can play with Roscoe, our Beagle."

"I've never had a dog," I said. "That sounds fun."

"Yes, yes," Rosemary said. "So, it's getting late and I'd like to get home." She turned to me. "Josey, I'll get you a bag tomorrow so you can pack up your stuff and go with Jack and Marcy Friday evening. Okay?"

"Okay," I said. I was full of jitters at the prospect of having a real home to live in, despite the fact it would be temporary. Rosemary and I were always at odds and I secretly longed to be away from her.

"You can return to your room then, Josey. I'll see you tomorrow."

I got up, waved goodbye to the Paars, and left the office with no idea what my time with them would be like.

And it only got worse. What little kindness that might have existed in my relationship with Rosemary ended after the knife fiasco. She never looked at me the same way again, like I had somehow smote her in the most disgusting way imaginable. And it wasn't subtle. She grounded me from extracurricular activities for a month after that, and I don't think I received a dessert at dinner time for two months. The air between us went cold that year, and our winter would last five more years.

23

I hit the road back to my motel and ponder whether I should tell Vick and Emily about my little run-in. The shit is getting pretty deep when people are sent after me with a good old-fashioned cease and desist knife threat. And considering there are less than ten people who even know where I'm at, this clearly came from someone within AWT. I'd give anyone three guesses as to who that someone is but they'd only need one. Her name starts with a Madame and ends with a K.

In the interest of our evolving trust-pact, I'm leaning toward sharing the truth with my team. Even though this incident has nothing to do with the mission at hand, the fact that it happened during my recon could represent a compromise of said mission. It doesn't, in my opinion, as this threat was a personal matter, but I don't think it would be fair to make that decision on my own.

Back at my room, I took a cold shower and am now lying in bed, looking at the ceiling and trying to envision what my life might be like in a few years. My mind veers easily to a scenario in which I'm not alive at all. I wonder if I should even pursue the truth of my past and my parents, especially considering the great personal risk in doing so. I remember I'm not alone in this endeavor. I have Ollie. I think I have the Dean and Dina, though they remain wildcards to some degree. When I reveal the whole truth to Vick and Emily, I truly believe they'll be on my side too. But Madame K is a powerful and deadly woman, and not someone to be taken lightly. She'd bury us all to save her own skin and keep the truth hidden.

Each day, I have to ask myself: is it worth it? Each day, I answer yes. I think the average person would do the same. Orphaned at five years old when my parents mysteriously disappeared. Left in the care of a woman in a completely different state. Given a false name and identity. And now, information has come to light that my parents may have been killed by the organization I now work for. Only one person seems to know the full truth about this, and she appears to be working diligently to keep it bottled up. Any reasonable person would go crazy knowing all this about themselves. To not do something would be choosing insanity. But no - straight jacket for me, thank you very much.

Physically, I'm fine, but mentally, I'm exhausted. I think I'll take a nap. Hopefully, when I wake up, I'll see a clear path forward and be ready to set the record straight with my team.

On my way to meet with the team, I stopped off at a real Texas BBQ joint and had the most mouthwatering ribs and brisket I've ever had the pleasure of eating. I'm now stuffed to the rafters. Ever since I started paying more attention to my fitness and doing the Parkour stuff, I eat a diet high in fat and protein with very little carbohydrates. Being in Texas has made that much easier and I kind of wish I lived here. I put so much meat down, the waitress was beginning to worry.

When I reach the parking lot, I see the van around the side of the building. There are other businesses in the area, but on a weeknight, it's relatively quiet.

I park about a hundred feet away and walk over. I knock four times on the rear doors. "It's Scissors."

The doors slowly open. I feel the rush of cool air blow by my face. My truck doesn't have air conditioning, which was a huge mistake, so I relish every opportunity to have some.

Vick puts a hand out, I accept it, and he pulls me into the van, closing the doors and locking them behind me.

Emily is sitting at a computer terminal but turns toward me. Vick and I join her in the other two chairs.

"So, what do ya got?" Vick asks me.

"Hopefully, just what we need to move this thing along. Tailing Denis this morning, I overheard a conversation he had with Gus about a private dinner they're having July 18th where they are supposed to discuss some Jackson house thing. They've gone so far as to reserve the back room of a restaurant, all to themselves. I assume they know the manager or the owner and can get ultimate privacy."

"Ooo, that's really good, Josey," Vick says. "That's just a week from now. Nice job."

"What's the restaurant?" Emily asks.

"Dawson's Steakhouse. Southeast edge of Houston, on the road to Galveston."

"Good," Emily says. She turns to the computer terminal next to her and starts typing. "I'll get maps and a rundown of the area so we can be fully prepped."

"So, what's our play here?" I ask. "Do we hit them at the restaurant or do we eavesdrop on the meeting and get more info on the Jackson house thing?"

"That's a good question," Vick answers. "It's hard to assume the Jackson house thing is related to the sex trafficking. Could be a wedding for all we know."

"That seems highly unlikely," I rebut.

"Maybe, but the restaurant wouldn't necessarily be a good place for the execution either. If the owner is helpful to them, that will make it hard. And you can bet your sweet ass they'll be heavily guarded."

"Yeah, so?"

"Contract is very specific. No collateral damage unless absolutely necessary. The fact that we're discussing it ahead of time means it's fully avoidable."

"Always a stickler for the rules," I say.

"Always a pain in the ass," Vick says.

"Play nice you two," Emily interjects without interrupting the work she's doing.

I run my hand over my head and through my hair, trying to think of an angle I can present that will at least make Vick consider the idea of a take down at Dawson's. I can't think of a single argument that will trump Vick's 'play it by the rules' approach.

"So, for arguments sake, should we just find a way to bug that room?" I ask. "Maybe then we can figure out if the Jackson house event is the one we've been waiting for?"

Truth be told, I'd rather hit the Jackson house anyway, especially if it turns out to be what I think it is. By framing it this way, I hope Vick will think of it as his idea. If I say too much about wanting to bust up the sex trafficking ring, he may shy away from it completely and I'll have gained nothing.

"Yeah, that's probably our best bet. I'll go over and check it out, pretend like I want to reserve the backroom, plant the bug."

Emily stands up and pulls open a cabinet door above her workstation. She sifts through a few of the items inside, then pulls something tiny out.

"Here, Vick," Emily says as she holds out her hand with the item held between her index finger and thumb. She drops it into his outstretched palm. "You're gonna want to use this."

"Damn that thing is small," I say.

"Oh yeah, but better than that, it's untraceable until we activate it, and we can do that remotely once the meeting is actually happening."

"In other words," Vick says, "if they do a sweep beforehand, they won't find it, right?"

"That is correct," Emily answers. "It's a new one the company created."

"Wow, that's awesome," I say.

Vick inspects the tiny device. It's clear on one side and black on the other. The black side is sticky for application purposes. The only thing I can think of to compare it to size-wise is a single oat. Impressive.

"I'll work on getting a building blueprint for the restaurant, maps of the area, and all that jazz," Emily says. "Get'em sent to your phone ASAP."

"Great," Vick says. He turns to me. "You okay just continuing the recon on Denis, just to make sure nothing changes?"

"No sweat. Well, actually, a lot of sweat. I bought a truck with no air conditioning."

"Are you insane?" Vick asks. "It's like the seventh circle of hell down here."

"I know, I know."

"So, go get something else."

"Too much hassle at this point. Hopefully, we'll be outta here in the next couple weeks anyway."

"If we're lucky. Anything can happen."

"Speaking of anything happening. We need to have a little talk about something that happened this morning."

Suddenly, Emily and Vick are fixed on me. Emily looks even more terrified than usual, Vick more curious.

"When I was listening in on Denis this morning, a guy put a knife to my throat and threatened me."

"What the hell?" Vick shouts. "Why didn't you say something earlier?"

"Because it wasn't mission related. I didn't want to create some kind of panic between us."

"So, what the heck happened?" Emily asks.

"He told me to drop the investigation and there'd be consequences if I didn't. Then he disappeared. That was it."

They're both puzzled, then at nearly the identical moment, it dawns on them what the threat meant.

Emily puts a hand to her mouth.

"Shit," Vick says. "I have to say, I've had my doubts about that whole mess, but this." He shakes his head. "What have you got yourself into, Josey?"

"It's not me! I didn't ask for this. I didn't go snooping around trying to bust this thing wide open. I was given information, and if you were in my shoes, you'd be doing the same damn thing, so don't fuckin' blame me for all this crap."

Vick doesn't respond. I can tell he's thinking about the truth behind my words. After a few moments, he nods.

"That may be, but in order for me to understand what you're doing, I need the whole story."

"Fair enough," I say. "Look, I still don't know the whole story myself, but I'm getting close. After this mission, I'm planning on another excursion to dig a little deeper. With every step I take, it gets more dangerous. Whatever it is, it's running parallel to a possible unraveling of the leadership at AWT, and probably because of it."

"I find that hard to believe," Vick says.

"I know. So do I. Nothing makes sense. But when we graduated from the academy, and I'm putting myself at great risk telling you guys this because I don't know where your true loyalty lies, but Ollie handed me a note that said, 'Do you want to know who you really are?' Then he whispered the name Allister Cole in my ear."

"That explains why you were acting so weird for weeks after," Emily says.

"Yeah. As you guys know, I was an orphan from age five when my parents disappeared. When I snuck out of the house recently, I went back to Randallstown Children's Home to try and get some info. Turns out, Rosemary Greenburg, the lady who ran the home while I was there, was found dead around the time we were graduating."

"Could've been a coincidence," Vick says.

"I thought of that, but after talking to Ollie, he told me Allister Cole wasn't a person, but a company, a coal company in Pennsylvania. He also discovered some information about Rosemary. Apparently, she met with someone in Pennsylvania, very near the headquarters of Allister Coal, two days before I came under her care. In AWT's files, Ollie found a contract for assassination for a woman and her husband. They worked for Allister Coal, some whistleblower thing. They had a child. All three disappeared without a trace the day before Rosemary went to Pennsylvania."

"Holy shit!" Emily says.

"I'm trying to piece this all together here," Vick says, "but are you saying that missing child is you?"

"We think so. I'm still looking into it. That's the second trip away from home I need to make. Pennsylvania. Poke around. See what I can dig up. Can you understand now why this is such a big deal for me, and why I have to be so careful?"

"God, yes," Vick says. "The implications of this. Jesus. I'm really sorry, Josey. I didn't know."

"How could you?"

"I know, but Jesus, I called Ollie when you left." Vick shakes his head. "I shouldn't have done that."

"It's okay, Vick. It really is. I get it. I don't like it, but I get it. We don't need to keep looking in the rearview mirror though. Let's just keep our eyes on the road because the road going forward is gonna be bumpy as hell."

"Agreed."

I suddenly notice Emily is crying, softly, trying hard to keep herself quiet.

"Emily, are you okay?" I ask.

Vick turns to her. "What's wrong?"

Emily wipes her face. "It's nothing. I mean ... I feel terrible. This is so fucked."

I don't know what to say. It is fucked. If I were to say anything else, it wouldn't be honest. I could say that it's going to be okay, but I don't know that. I could tell her not to worry, but she most certainly should worry. Ugh. I'm having regrets about sharing. The last thing I ever wanted to do was get others involved, and thus, put them in harm's way.

"I wish I could tell you guys this will be alright but it might not be. There's a pretty good chance I'm gonna end up in a body bag. I'll try to keep you two as far away from it as possible, so you don't end up in one too."

Emily bursts into tears, covering her face with both hands to muffle it.

Vick puts his left arm around her and rubs her back.

"I have to get outta here," Emily blurts. She turns away from Vick, gets out of her chair, and bolts to the front of the van. She grabs a drawstring leather bag from the front seat and exits the van using the driver-side door.

I make a move to follow her but Vick stops me.

"Let her go. She needs some time to think. She'll be fine."

"I don't know, Vick. We can't have her coming unhinged at this point in the mission. We're almost at the finish line."

"I know. I know." Vick rubs the light brown stubble of his cheeks and chin with his left hand. "Let me think."

I've become quite fond of Emily. I won't deny it. She's good at the hacker thing and a valuable asset to the team. On the personal side, she's easy to talk to and is a genuinely caring person. Her continued erratic and emotional behavior the last few months has put all of that into perspective for me. I know it has for Vick as well. If we get through this mission without a total collapse on Emily's part and her current state of mind doesn't improve soon, we'll have no choice but to report her behavior to the company. Not doing so would be irresponsible and dangerous.

"Why don't you head over to the area where that restaurant is, get a look around, take a few pictures for me, then get some rest. As soon as Emily has all the other details, I'll pop over there and plant the bug."

"Should I talk to Emily first?"

"I'll talk to her. If she can't get her mind right, I'll let you know."

"Go easy on her," I plea. "Whatever she's dealing with, it's tearing her apart."

"I will. I want her to succeed. I want this team to succeed. But if she can't get her shit together, and soon, it'll be out of our hands."

"I know." I sigh. "I'm gonna take off then. I'll email you anything I find down there."

"Stay safe out there. And if anything unusual happens again, please tell me right away. I can't do this mission

without you."
    "I will. Thanks."

24

Wednesday, July 18th

Emily finally calmed down enough to get back to work. Vick told me he had a real heart-to-heart with her and she seemed to respond well. She agreed to have a long and deep conversation with Dina when the mission was over, even if that ultimately meant she would have to leave the team. Vick made it clear how much we cared for her as a person and a teammate, and that we wanted her to stay, but her behavior was intolerable considering the kind of work we do. If she wouldn't get the help she needed of her own volition, we'd have no choice but to make the decision for her. She promised to do so as soon as we return to New York.

Back at it, Emily provided Vick with all the data regarding the restaurant layout, surrounding area traffic patterns, even the name of the manager and his assistant managers. I also gave Vick the pictures of the area, as he requested, so all he needed to do was make a trip down there.

Vick had no trouble placing the bug at Dawson's Restaurant. He showed up right at eleven a.m. as they were opening. He spoke directly to the day shift manager to inquire about having a small family reunion in their private dining room area. They were very accommodating and took him straight away to show off the space.

The large square room was dimly lit, full of Texas cattle ranch atmosphere, which included large wood beams across the ceiling, bullhorn chandeliers, and various antique metal tools of the trade. There were three doors. One in from the hostess area, a door with direct access to the kitchen, and an emergency exit.

There were two large corner booths flanking four smaller booths along the back wall, all with dark brown wood tables and dark burgundy booth seats. The rest of the room was filled with four-seater square tables with barrel-shaped wood chairs. It was obvious to Vick that the far-left corner booth is where someone like Gus Taggert would do business. It was the furthest point from any door and one could see the entire room from that spot.

Vick casually walked the room, the manager in tow. When he reached the far-left corner booth, he turned around to face the room, his butt touching the edge of the table. He pretended to look around the room, analyzing the space for his imaginary family reunion. With the bug between the index finger and thumb of his left hand, Vick reached as far under the table as he could without it being obvious. He guessed it was eight inches back from the edge. Far enough not to be easily spotted or wiped off during a casual cleaning.

Satisfied, Vick walked the manager back to the hostess area and shared that he would have to check with his wife before making a final decision, assuring that he'd call the next day to book the space.

The Kill Team is now sitting in the van parked a couple of blocks away from Dawson's Restaurant. I placed a sticky-cam on a light pole in the parking lot so we could monitor the comings and goings once Gus and Denis were inside. After that, I walked up and down the sidewalk across the street from the restaurant until they arrived at 1:30 p.m.

They came in separate vehicles, Denis in his Mercedes, Gus in his Rolls Royce driven by his main chauffeur, Michael Dudley, a middle-aged white man, dressed in the typical black and white chauffeur duds. A third vehicle, a black Suburban, followed the Rolls in. Two rather intimidating, large, well-dressed men came out of that SUV and entered the restaurant before anyone else, returning to the parking lot nearly five minutes later. They had no doubt swept the entire place for security issues. Denis and Gus appeared satisfied with the report and went in alone. The two muscle-men stood guard outside, one near the Rolls, the other standing about ten feet from the front door.

After witnessing all that, I returned to the van, joining Vick and Emily to watch the outside camera, but more importantly, listen to their conversation. Upon my return, Emily activated the listening device, putting the audio through to the speaker system of the van. Her computer was also recording the audio for later scrutiny.

Now we listen...

Manager: Get you gentlemen the usual pot of coffee, lots of cream, lots of sugar?

There is a shuffling sound, like the men are scooting into their seats in the booth.

Denis: Yes.

Gus: Thank you, Aaron.

Manager: Great. Be right back.

A minute passes with nothing.

Gus: How's tricks?

Denis: Couldn't be better. How's Margaret?

Gus: Wouldn't know. Fine I assume. She's in Venice with some girlfriends. Probably won't see her for a month.

Denis: Never saw much point in being married. You know that. I like to keep it simple.

Gus: To each his own my friend.

We can hear the coffee pot and cups hitting the table.

Manager: There you go gents. Can I get you anything else?

Gus: That'll be all, thank you.

Denis: Yeah, just give us some privacy for a while. Maybe check on us in fifteen to twenty minutes, see if we need more coffee.

Manager: Will do.

There's a rapping of knuckles on the table.

Manager: Enjoy.

We can hear spoons rattling in coffee mugs. Sipping.

Denis: I know we've had this conversation before, but I'd much rather we discuss the Jackson house thing in your office. Anyone could be listening.

Gus: I spend too much time in my office as it is. Besides, should something ever go down, I don't want that shit anywhere near my real business. You know how it is. The Feds, the SEC, the IRS, they're always snooping around. Comes with the territory.

Denis: I know. Just feel so exposed out here. I don't like taking chances.

Gus: Nothing to worry about. My men checked it out. The Feds don't care much to watch me eating a steak or drinking coffee. Your concerns are duly noted, as always.

Denis: So, the Jackson house.

Gus: Yes.

Denis: I have people making the usual preparations. The invites have already been sent and RSVP'd, through the usual secure channels.

Gus: Good. How about turnout?

Denis: Most of the usual suspects, a few new ones.

Gus: And ... the merchandise?

Denis: All set. About two-thirds Mexican girls, the rest from here.

Gus: How young?

Denis: A few sixteen, seventeen. Most under twenty-four. You'll get first look, same as always.

Gus: I want you down there the day before anyone arrives. You're the only man I trust to ensure complete privacy and security.

Denis: That's why you pay me the big bucks. But of course. It'll be perfect or it won't be at all.

Gus: Good.

Denis: I have to make a quick trip up to Dallas this weekend, so I won't likely see you again until the twenty-seventh. I'll get back home on Tuesday, then I'll go down there Wednesday to supervise the finishing touches.

Gus: Sounds like you have it under control.

They go on for another thirty minutes, talking about other business dealings, Texas and national politics, the financial markets, and Gus Taggert's need for a high-tech upgrade at some of his office buildings and the amount of money it will cost to do it. They drink two full pots of coffee and both use the restroom before settling their bill. Gus left first, his security SUV in tow. Denis came out of the building ten minutes later and actually drove past us on his way to some unknown location.

By this point, we have most of the information we need, and I'm fuming, even some time after. That part of our targets' brazen conversation about underage girls made it difficult to keep my emotions in check at the time, but now I'm about to go full-on Mount St. Helens.

"Fuck these fuckin' guys!" I say. "We can't let that little rendezvous happen. We just can't."

"Cool down, Josey," Vick commands. "I heard the same thing you did, and believe me, I don't like it one bit. But our job here is to take out Gus and Denis, not break up a sex ring."

"Oh, that's bullshit!" I can't keep myself from shouting. "There's gonna be a bunch of sinister motherfuckers there. We can take'em all out as far as I'm concerned."

Vick rises from his chair, hovering large over me. "We will do no such thing goddamn it!"

I stand up, throw my chair aside, and get right in Vick's face. "I'll call the cops then, give'em an anonymous tip. That'll shut that shit down."

"You do that, I'll shoot you myself."

"Come on guys. This is not helping," Emily says. She leaves her chair and uses her arms to put a little space between Vick and myself. "Think about it, Josey. Why are we here? To kill Gus and Denis. When they're dead, that sex ring falls apart. They run it, clearly. No Gus, no more Jackson place."

I ponder her words and they make sense.

"Good point, Emily," Vick says, sitting back down. "We do our job, the rest will handle itself."

Reluctantly, I pull my chair back to me and flop down in it. I stare at the monitor still showing the parking lot of the restaurant.

"Can you at least concede me one thing?" I ask.

"Maybe," Vick replies.

"Once the job is done, let me get the girls out of there, on my own. You guys don't have to be involved at all. That way, if the company finds out, it's all on me. Please let me do that."

I can tell by his expression that he doesn't want to say yes. I give him my best look of desperation and mouth the word please.

"Fine. I'm not heartless, ya know. I told you guys why I had to leave the F.B.I., what happened. I don't want a repeat. But let me be perfectly fuckin' clear. The mission to take out Gus and Denis is the only priority. If you can easily rescue the girls, safely, and I don't mean for them, I mean for you and us, then do it. Otherwise, we get the hell outta dodge and don't look back."

"Okay."

"I mean it, Josey."

"I got it."

"Good, then let's figure out what we're going to do here."

25

Wednesday Morning, July 25th

We're on our way to the Jackson house, following Denis from his home in Houston. We have no idea where the hell this place is, so we're flying blind here. The best we can tell is that the location is somewhere in Jackson County, which wouldn't be too far from Houston, and it's definitely rural. This mission could easily go up in smoke over the next few days if this turns out to be anything but the perfect locale for finishing the job.

As a precaution, we have decided to take two vehicles. I'm in the mini-van Vick was using to get around Texas. Sweet, sweet air conditioning. I ditched my shitty truck, handing the keys and the title over to a couple of Mexican day laborers outside The Home Depot. Emily and Vick are in the big van doing the actually tailing for now. We'll switch off from time to time, just to mix it up.

Right now, I'm a few cars back of the van on Route 59, dreading a phone call I need to make. I want to tell Ollie about the knife incident, in case there's been an escalation at HQ. What I don't want is for Ollie to use this incident as any kind of fuel for action. It was a threat and I wasn't harmed. I can't justify any retaliation at this point.

When we reach the southwest side of El Campo, Denis

stops at a gas station. We pull off onto a side road just before the gas station and turn around so we can have full view of him when he leaves. Denis proceeds to pump gas and I finally decide it's time to make my call.

"Hey."

"Everything okay?" Ollie asks. He's not expecting to hear from me. The team is on a mission. Unless we need help with something, it's generally frowned upon to make contact with anyone.

"Fuckin' peaches."

"If this is mission related, you're going to have to call The Dean. I'm on, uh ... vacation."

"Oh. Okay. But no, it's not about the mission. Something happened. Something that is probably going to piss you off, like royally."

"Well shit, Josey. Don't bury the lead. What happened? You're not hurt, are you?"

He's genuinely concerned, and not just the looking out for a coworker kind of concerned.

"I'm fine. I was not hurt in anyway, other than maybe my pride. I was doing recon recently and a guy put a knife to my throat, threatened me, told me to quit the investigation. That was it. Then he disappeared. I think we both know what that's about."

"Fuckin' bitch!"

"Hey!"

"Not you. She's completely on to us, not that I should've expected less."

"So, what does this mean for us?" I see Denis leave the gas pump and go into the station. I don't have much time.

"It means our suspicions are true and she clearly has something to hide regarding you. Whatever it is, it's apparently worth killing over."

"What should we do?"

"Finish your mission, then we need to have talk about all this. There's something I need to tell you but I don't want to do it over the phone."

"Well, Jesus! That's a helluva tease."

'We'll continue this conversation when you're done."

"I'm getting a kind of sick feeling about this, Ollie."

"Me too. Keep your eyes and ears open, even wider than usual, if that's possible. Still in Texas, I take it?"

"Yes. And I will. I won't let a motherfucker sneak up on me like that again, that's for sure."

"Just be careful. We'll talk when you get back. I gotta go."

"You be careful too.'"

"I will. Bye."

The line goes dead before I can say anything else. And just in time. Denis has returned to his car and is getting ready to pull away.

We're back on Denis' trail, continuing down 59. I'm in the lead now. We're getting close to Jackson County, so having me on the tight follow in the mini-van will be less noticeable then the bigger van. We expect to leave the main road and end up on country ones as we zero in on the final location, one that will likely be rural and remote.

I'm trying hard to focus but I keep drifting back to Ollie's little tease. Does he have more information to share about my past or something else, and if so, what? For him to want to wait and tell me in-person means it must be pretty big.

After another thirty minutes on the road, Denis and the secret caravan that follows take a turn onto a road heading north into Jackson County. It appears our hunch about that is coming true. Traffic in the area is next to nothing, so we need to be extra careful. Denis is about a half-mile ahead of me. When he turns off to his destination, we'll drive right on by. Emily will use the GPS to get exact satellite coordinates so we won't lose the spot and can do some research. Not that we'll find much. Depending on how old the place is, there might not be any blueprints filed, and even if there are, there will no doubt have been major unpermitted renovations.

The drive through the country is pleasant but boring. Most

of the landscape is thirsty grasslands and sections of heavily treed acres. There's a farmhouse and related buildings here and there, and I've spotted several manmade lakes. Emily told me there's a good chance of rain today too. When the land down here is as parched as it is, flash floods are a concern. Add another potential obstacle to the list.

Forty-five minutes after leaving Route 59, Denis starts to slow down. Even this far back, I can tell. I'm suddenly gaining on him. My heart starts racing. I steady myself with controlled breathing. This mission is creeping closer to conclusion, yet there seems to be a palatable sharpness in the air, and not fear, more like dread. I'm having trouble discerning whether this feeling stems from the mission or my own bullshit. Either way, I'm uncomfortable.

I come over a small hill and see Denis turn off the road and down what looks like a gravel driveway.

I get on my phone.

"Rock, this is Scissors, target is turning off the road. Pull off."

"Copy that. Pulling off the road."

"I'm going to do a drive by. Hang tight."

I keep Vick on the line and continue down the road at fifty-five miles per hour. When I reach the place Denis turned off, I glance over and see the dusty trail he went down. It's not a true driveway or a road. It's unmarked and looks like it goes for about two hundred feet before turning sharply to the left into a grove of trees too dense for me to see anything from the road. I drive another mile before I stop on the side of the road.

"Rock, there's a dusty road, more like a trail just before a bunch of trees. You can't see shit from the road."

"Roger that, Scissors."

"It's exactly one mile south of my current location. I'm going to take a few pictures from here, so give me a minute then meet me up the road."

"Roger that."

I end the call and reach over to the passenger seat where I

have a digital camera equipped with a telephoto lens. I grab it and get out of the van. From the ditch side of the van, I point the camera and zoom all the way in on the grove of trees. It runs even deeper than I thought it would but I can see a small clearing about a quarter of a mile in. Just past that, I can only assume there is a building but I can't make anything out from here. I snap a few pictures then turn the camera to the road and take a few more.

Back on the phone, "Tell Paper we need satellite shots of this area. I can't see shit through the trees. It's too far back and I'm too far away."

"Already on it."

"I'm getting back in the car. Go ahead and catch up. I'll follow you guys out of here."

"Roger that."

Later in the day

After finding the Jackson County location, Emily spent hours digging, researching, and analyzing. I don't think she stopped to take a sip of her soda for three hours. I tried to talk to her a few times but she kept waving me off and shushing me.

Finally, after making us stew for an uncomfortably long afternoon, she sits Vick and I down in the van near 7 p.m. to reveal what she had found. We're sitting in the parking lot of a BBQ restaurant in Victoria.

"Okay, here's what we have," Emily says, her laptop in front of her on a stool. "The most recent information I could find on the property is from ten years ago. At that time, the property contained a house, a detached three-car garage, and eighteen acres of land."

"Big place," I say.

"Yeah. Well, it was purchased for one hundred fifty thousand dollars by a company called F.T.A. Incorporated. I couldn't find jack-shit on that company other than it was created six months before the purchase of the home, and the two listed officers must be fake because I couldn't find anything about them either, anywhere. Very shady."

"Sounds like we have a winner, location wise," Vick says. "For us and for them."

I nod.

"It gets worse," Emily says. "The only blueprints of the buildings I could find are from thirty-five years ago. There have been no permits granted from the county since then. In other words, this place could be completely different from when it was purchased ten years ago."

"Shit. That's not good," I say.

"What can we do?" Vick asks. "Be a little hard to plan a mission without any building details."

"Plus, whatever is there, we have no idea what kind of security might be in place," I say.

Emily reaches to her left and pulls a blue plastic tote from under the console and pops the lid off, throwing it aside. From inside, she removes a white drone, about two feet across on all sides. Affixed to the bottom is a complicated looking metal box about the size of a coffee cup. One side of that metal box has two camera lenses imbedded.

"Let me introduce you to the White Dragon."

"Me likey," I say.

"I didn't even know we had that," Vick adds.

"We have a lot of tech you guys probably don't know about," Emily says. "This bad boy will take 4K, 3-D images from several hundred feet up, is whisper quiet, has a range of about one mile, and it can even detect heat signatures, including electrical lines and humans."

"Whoa. That's awesome," Vick says. "Do you know how to fly that thing? Because I sure as hell don't."

"I do. We trained with these things."

"How come you never mentioned them before now?" I ask.

"Haven't really needed to until now."

"Well, fuck me, that thing could save us a ton of time from now on," I say.

"We're supposed to use it sparingly, especially in the city. It has top secret tech on it. Out here, it's a great option. In the city, not so much."

"Fine," I say, dejected.

Vick picks the device up and begins inspecting the underbelly. "It's fairly lightweight, considering. You said you can operate this thing from a mile away?"

"Yep," Emily answers.

"It wouldn't happen to have night vision, would it?" Vick asks.

"You betcha," Emily says as her eyes light up. "In fact, I think we should go there tonight and do a fly-over, get some footage, test out the sensors. That way we have something to study until we can take it up during the day tomorrow. What do you guys think?

"We still have almost two hours of daylight," I say. "So, how about we go in and get some grub first? The smell of this place is killing me right now."

"Great idea," Vick says. "I haven't had anything to eat all day except a couple of handfuls of almonds."

"I could eat," Emily says. Vick hands her the drone and she carefully places it back in the tote, replaces the lid, and slides it back where it came from.

I jump from my chair. "Awww yeeeah. I'm 'bout to destroy some ribs y'all."

Inside the restaurant

Our table is full of family-style food plates. Ribs, brisket, cornbread, barbeque shredded pork, baked beans, mashed potatoes, and southern green beans. I won't be touching anything but the meat, of course.

The interior of this place is clean and made for quick eats. The tablecloths are plastic red and white checkered, there are shiny aluminum napkin holders, a selection of barbeque sauces, bowls of moist towelettes on every table, and the soda is unlimited self-serve.

We've killed about half the food on the table and have barely spoken, and for the first time since we've been in Texas, not a single word about the mission. It's not an uncomfortable silence, more like a quiet reprieve from chaos. Emily has been all about the business at hand since Vick spoke to her, and that almost worries me. She's currently on her third wine cooler, and for anyone who knows her, that's not far from being blitzed. She's masking, bottling up her troubles. If she ends up exploding, hopefully it will be after we get back home. If it happens before then, we could all end up dead.

The more immediate problem is that once it's dark out, she has to pilot that drone. The large amount of barbeque in her should help offset the booze, but she is kind of a lightweight. Time to cut her off.

Just as I'm about to speak, Vick gets up.

"I gotta hit the head," he says, promptly leaving the table.

I say nothing to him and look back to Emily.

"How you feeling, Em?"

She looks up from inspecting the little bits of brisket still left on her plate. "What? Oh. Fine. Why?"

"Well, ya know, we need you clear-headed so you can fly that drone in a bit."

"No problem. I've only had," she stops and picks up her wine cooler bottle and gives it a few shakes, "two and a half of these. No problem at all."

I try and get a good look at her eyes. They're not glassy or bloodshot. If she stops drinking now, she'll be fine.

"Good. Good."

I want her to open up to me but I'm not sure this is the best time to do it. Maybe some light probing.

"You know you can talk to me, right? About anything. And I don't mean as a co-worker, I mean as a friend."

"I'm not sure we are friends."

I scowl. I'm not sure how to respond. Is she fucking with me?

"Really? That's news to me."

She sighs. "What I mean is, I don't know if it's such a good idea to have friends in this company, in this business."

"I admit, it's complicated, but I don't think it's impossible."

"I think I've figured out it's better just to be alone, not have people you care about. Because eventually, you'll just end up hurting the people you love, and in this business, it's almost guaranteed to end up bloody."

"That's crazy talk."

"No, it's not, Josey. It's most definitely not."

"I grant you, there's an inherent level of danger in this work, but I don't think that means we can't have interpersonal relationships."

"When people trust you, they let down their guard. There's nothing good about that."

"I really don't know what you're talking about." I'm regretting even starting this conversation. It's killing my confidence in her. If I were forced to make a snap judgement right now about her ability to perform and stay on the team, I'm leaning toward giving her the boot. Damn it.

"You will. Mark my words. One day you will."

I'm surprised at the coldness of her words, and that she's not crying. The wine coolers must be doing a number on her. Either that or she's just found a way to compartmentalize and build a nice little wall. If this is a new Emily that we have to look forward to, I'm not a fan. Sweet Emily, caring Emily, I like. Crass Emily, defensive Emily, I can do without.

Vick returns from the bathroom to break up the conversation. Good. It was going down the drain, fast. He senses the awkwardness.

"Everything okay?" he asks as he takes his seat.

Emily chugs the rest of her drink and slams the bottle down on the table. "Things are great. I'm ready to get that drone in the air. How about you guys?"

Vick can sense the fake exuberance the same as I can but he doesn't challenge it. I decide not to inform him of the details of our odd little chat. We're so close to finishing this mission, everything going as well as it can, yet it seems to be balancing on the razor's edge known as Emily's emotional state.

Vick glances my way. I give him my best shit-eating grin in an effort to deter him. "Let's fly that fucker," I say with the same tone as Emily.

Vick rolls his eyes.

At least now he doesn't think something is wrong.

26

Wednesday Night

About a mile down the road from the Jackson house, we found a driveway that leads to a small lake and an abandoned mobile home. Parked a little way back from the road, we are practically hidden. This position is where we've decided to have the big van, not just for tonight's test flight, but for the main event as well. Even though I'm here now with the mini-van, I'll actually be parked a mile down the road in the other direction tomorrow night. Safer to be in different locations in case we are discovered.

Vick and I are seated inside the van with our eyes locked on a monitor showing a POV of the drone camera. The backdoors are wide open and Emily is standing right there on the outside with the controller in her hands. There is a five-inch full color monitor attached to the top of that controller.

Emily guides the drone to the property, staying just high enough for the trees not to be a bother, yet low enough for high quality, fine detail, closeup images and video. She's using the night-vision with heat signature and electrical overlay as there are only two lights on outside of the house. One is on the front porch, the other on the front of the garage, just above the garage door.

"See the three reddish orange dots," Emily says. "Those

are people in the house. The lighter colored one in the far-left corner is someone probably in the basement. That's why it's fainter. If someone was on the second floor, they'd be darker."

"Cool," I say. "I take it the yellow lines are the electrical lines?"

"Yep," Emily answers. "So, we've got a two-story house with a full basement, and there appears to be an extension of the basement that leads to the garage."

"Backup entrance or escape tunnel," Vick says.

"Safe bet," I add.

There are two vehicles outside. One is Denis's Mercedes, the other is a dark colored sedan. We know the house is being prepped for a big event, so the other two people are likely a cleaning crew or other staff.

As the drone circles around the perimeter of the buildings, we note the house has two exterior doors, front and back. The garage has only the large garage door made for a two-car garage.

"Based on these electrical readings, I don't think there's a real security system, and certainly no cameras on the property. That's good for us."

"Yes, it is," Vick says.

"There is, however, what looks like pass code entry locks on both house doors and the garage. They're likely just the deadbolt kind. You'll have to bust them to get in but they won't sound an alarm or anything."

The person in the basement comes upstairs and the three of them gather near the front door. They may be leaving. We watch Emily bring the drone around from the back of the house and settle on a shot of where the two vehicles are parked. We see two of the three people leave the house, put a few items in the trunk of the sedan, then get in the car and leave the property.

"Should I follow them?" I ask Vick.

"No. If Denis leaves, I'm going in and I'll need you here to assist."

"Okay."

"Emily, do we have more of those undetectable audio bugs?" Vick asks.

"Yes. See that gray little box on the top shelf? They're in there."

Vick rises, finds the box, and pulls it down. From inside, he removes three of the devices and places them on the lower desk next to the computer keyboard. He returns to his chair.

My eyes are locked on the dark orange dot known as Denis Koplen. I want so bad to taser that son of bitch, duct tape him to a chair, and horse whip him until he cries and begs me to stop. Then I'll just hook his testicles up to a car battery and work on him some more. There's nothing in the contract that says we can't torture these guys first. But damn it, this is Vick's mission and I'm at his mercy. I know he won't allow it, so I won't even suggest it. Doesn't mean I can't fantasize.

Suddenly, the exterior lights of the house go dark and out walks Denis through the front door. Hopefully, he's leaving for the night. This will allow Vick to do some indoor recon and plant the audio devices. We could certainly use some detailed pictures of the interior layout.

Emily backs the drone away a few hundred feet but zooms the camera in, that way if it happens to fall out of the sky, Denis won't see or hear anything.

We watch Denis as he gets in his car, does what looks like sending a few text messages, and then he drives off the property and down the road, away from us. We have no idea if he'll return this evening, so Vick pops out of his chair and chooses a rifle to take with him. He already has handguns strapped to his ankle and his waste. He pockets the audio devices, pats himself down to check for his phone, puts an earpiece in so we can communicate with him, then scoots past me and out of the back of the van.

"I'm going in."

"How are you going to get in?" I ask.

"I'll find a window to crawl through."

"And when that doesn't work?" I continue badgering.

"I'll figure it out, damn it! This might be our only chance of getting inside."

I look back at the monitor. "Em, how much more time can you be in the air with that thing?"

"I'm bringing it back to put a different battery in."

"I'm gonna run straight across the properties to get there," Vick says. "Shouldn't take me too long. Have the dragon back over to the house by the time I get there. I'll need you to keep an eye out to alert me if anyone shows up."

"I will," Emily says.

"Be careful," I say but I'm not sure Vick even hears me as he's already off and running, his rifle out in front to use the attached light as a guide. I plug a headset into our tiny soundboard, put them on my ears, and reposition the mic in front of my face.

A few minutes later, Emily enters the van with the drone in her hands. She quickly finds a new battery, exchanges it, and is right back outside with the dragon in flight.

The sudden departure of Denis and Vick has my pulse going and my palms sweating. Well, that could be the humidity, but either way, this shit is getting real. At some point in the next forty-eight hours, we'll likely be executing another contract, our most tricky one to date, one that feels like the stakes are higher for reasons I can't quite put my finger on. There are two targets, so yeah, that adds a little challenge. There is also the added tension of possibly breaking up a sex trafficking outfit and the fragility of Emily's emotional state. I just don't think those things are what's bothering me. Whatever it is, it remains clouded and distant in my mind. We are well-trained and work hard to consider every facet of danger and risk. I don't like this scratching at the back of my head. My instincts for impending peril are rarely wrong.

"Testing, testing. Get back to me, Rock," I say.

"Copy that, Scissors. Loud and clear."

"Watch your step out there. Could be any number of fox

holes or whatever. You twist your ankle, I'm leaving your ass out there."

"Roger that," Vick responds. "But no, you won't. You want these fuckers dead as much as I do."

"Copy that," I say.

"I'm about halfway there. I'll let you know when I reach the house."

"Copy that." I turn to Emily. "He's almost there. Where's the drone?"

"Already there. Check the monitor. I'm scouting out the driveway."

I confirm what she said. If any lights show up from that direction, we'll know a car is coming down the drive. Now we just have to hope Vick can find an easy way into the house or this is going to be the shortest recon exercise in history.

A few minutes later, I hear Vick's voice in my ear.

"Paper and Scissors, I'm at the house. Going around to the back to see if I can find a loose window. Copy."

"Copy that, Rock," I say. We wait for what seems like ten minutes but it's really only been three.

"I was able to jimmy open a window on the back of the house. I'm in the dining room. Copy."

"Copy that," I say. "We have eyes on the drive. Stay vocal with us. Tell us what you see."

"Roger that. The interior is very modern, brand new looking. Compared to the shitty exterior, this place is a palace. Everything is brown and white. I'm seeing a small kitchen. Heading through a doorway. Opens to a giant room. There are chairs all around the outside, nothing in the center. Showcase room for the girls?"

"Makes sense," I answer.

"Heading to the front of the house. There's a parlor, kind of an elegant entryway, small sitting areas on both sides. Going back to the big room to plant a bug."

Vick tells us he planted the bug, found a bathroom under the stairs, and is heading up to the second floor. There he discovers three doors. Two of them lead to empty rooms that look like they might have been bedrooms originally. They're on the front of the house. The other door leads to a large room on the back of the house, so big that Vick believes it must have been two or three other rooms in the past and was combined into one. There is a private bathroom off that room as well. The décor is classic Victorian with cherry furniture, velvety side chairs, and a canopied king bed with minimal bedding. There is a cart in the corner with decanters of varying alcoholic beverages, glasses, and an ice bucket.

The bathroom is white and gray marble with a six-foot, two-person jetted tub, double vanity, toilet, and heated towel rack. There are two white robes hanging on the back of the door. It is fully supplied with every toiletry and over-the-counter med a person could need. From cotton swabs to disposable razors to aspirin to shampoo, nothing is left to chance. Vick places a bug on the top of the bathroom door jamb, on the bedroom side.

It's pretty clear to us that Gus Taggert will be in that presidential suite for the events of Friday evening. Based on the conversations we've heard, it appears as though Denis does not partake and is basically a well-paid logistical manager. Personally, I find it hard to believe he wouldn't, but then again, he's never been married, has no kids, and as far as we can tell, no women in his life at all. Perhaps he's gay. That might explain it. Hadn't thought about that before now. Doesn't give him a pass. Whether a person participates or facilitates, they are the same in my book.

Vick finally goes down to the basement. He's working fast.

"The space is nicely finished, dark woods and wallpaper. There are eight small rooms, each about eight-foot square. A small bed, nightstand, chair in the corner. Each door has a gold number on it. There are four small bathrooms too, shared, obviously. There's a room at the end, not too big. Has about ten folding chairs in there. I'm going to put the last bug in here."

"Rock, I really want you to burn this fucking place to the ground," I say.

"Copy that. Continuing to the end of the hallway. There's a door. I'm going in. Uhhh, it's a long hallway, concrete, florescent lights overhead. I feel like I'm going away from the house toward the garage. There's a simple wooden staircase leading to another door. Paper, can you turn the drone over to here and verify my location? See if I'm at the locked door inside the garage?"

"Roger that," Emily responds. "Hang on a sec."

Emily maneuvers the drone to above the garage. I can see on the monitor Vick's heat signature and the electrical readout of the keypad lock.

"Rock, you are at the door inside the garage," Emily says.

"Copy that. Heading back to the house, then out the backdoor. That way I don't have to crawl out the window. I'll reset the deadbolt."

"Be quick, Rock," I say. "We've been hanging around too long and need to get the hell outta here."

"On my way," Vick says.

"I'm going to follow you back with the drone," Emily says.

I watch Vick leave the house and take basically the same path back to us. The drone stays directly over him.

When he arrives at the van, he is drenched with sweat. He jumps in the van and puts away the rifle.

"I'm sure glad I didn't send you in there," Vick says.

"Yeah."

I can hear Emily landing the drone and fussing with it.

"Let's just focus on the mission," Vick says as he takes off his tactical vest, throwing it behind the driver's seat. "Having been in there and seen that bullshit, I fully intend to shut it down, but we're going to do it my way."

"Good." I'm so happy to hear him say that. "You're Point. I'll follow your lead."

Emily joins us, drone in hand. "So, what do you think, Vick? Any chance this is the time and place?"

"Definitely. Is it perfect? No. Are we going to have a better chance than this to nab both of them? I doubt it. It just might not be as clean as the client would like."

Vick takes a seat as Emily puts the drone back in its tote. I take the headset off and disconnect it. Emily removes a bottled water from a small cooler on the floor and hands it to Vick, then sits down with us.

"Here's how I see it," Vick says before twisting open the water bottle, drinking half of it, then placing it on the floor next to his chair. From off the wall behind the console, he grabs a clipboard that has notebook paper and a pencil on it. He draws a square at the center, smaller square an inch away, then two ovals on opposite sides, near the edges of the paper. He writes HOUSE in the big square, GARAGE in the little square, SCISSORS in the left oval, PAPER in the right one.

"Josey, we'll have you in the mini-van here." He points to the left oval. "With a laptop, listening in, ready to act if needed. I want you fully armed and ready to run at me.

"Emily, we'll have you where we're at right now." He points to the other oval. "I'll need the drone in the air, but not too close. I'll need you to tag Denis' heat signature and keep an eye on him. I'll get in through the back door. If it's guarded, he's going down, nothing I can do about that. Otherwise, I'll just shatter the lock with nitrogen and get in.

"Once inside, I'll go straight upstairs and take out Gus. From there, I'll use his phone to text Denis and ask him to come up to the room to help with something. When he shows up, POP!"

"What about the girls?" I ask.

"I'm getting there. For Gus and Denis, I'll set up a murder suicide thing and leave the gun on Denis. Then, after I'm out and we're on the road, I'll let you call the police and report suspicious activity at the location. That's the best we can do here."

I ponder his plan. I don't like the idea of not personally freeing the women. There's no guarantee that the men and guards left behind won't dispose of them once the cops arrive. Then again, we'd likely have to kill all those men and guards to cover our own asses. How would we cover that up if the cops were called? If we didn't call the cops, how would we get the girls to safety and keep our identities secure? There are no good options here. Fuckity fuck.

"I wish there was a way to free the women ourselves, but I don't see how that will be possible, so I like your plan," I say. "It's better than nothing. Thank you for at least doing that."

"No matter what you might think of me, I'm not a monster."

"I know you're not," I say. "I've never thought that. I'm just more of a bend it 'til it breaks kind of girl, whereas you're a guy who always follows the thousand-page rulebook. An argument could be made for both."

"I can admit that," Vick says.

"Glad to see you two getting along," Emily adds. "I like the plan, if you want my input."

"Good. I think that's it then," Vick says. "Let's get outta here. We can come back tomorrow and do a few more flyovers, follow Denis around a bit, just to make sure nothing changes."

We part ways driving in opposite directions. Rather than go all the way back to Houston, we agree to stay close by. I drive two towns away and find a seedy motel to crash at for the night. Vick and Emily do the same, but since they are sharing a vehicle, Emily will drop Vick off a little way down the road from the motel they'll both be staying at. Vick will then wait for twenty minutes as Emily gets checked in, then he'll walk up and do the same.

27

Ollie sips on a glass of scotch and soda from the balcony of his hotel room in Colorado Springs, the lake below him shimmering in the midday sun. The 5-star resort affords Ollie some much needed downtime, although at every turn, it seems something from work creeps back into his life.

The deal he was sent to handle took less than forty-eight hours. He called Madame K and was subsequently ordered to take a break from work, get a massage, do some golfing. When the call ended, he threw his phone against the wall so hard it left a dent and shattered into twenty pieces.

A few weeks later, he was getting bored with Colorado and thinking about a trip to some exotic beach, even imagining Josey by his side. And as if the image of her in his mind had brought her forth, she called.

The news of her being at knifepoint and being threatened infuriated him. Madame K was on to their little game and had made another move of her own, this time more overt than having Rosemary Greenburg killed. That act was a coverup, this recent threat was a deterrent. If they continued their investigation, they wouldn't be playing with fire anymore, they'd be throwing gas on it and jumping in.

Before things got any deeper, however, Ollie knew he would have to come clean about how much he knew of Josey's parentage before she even came to the academy. He and Dina were well aware that AWT had taken a contract to kill Josey's mother. That information was shared by the Dean as part of the vetting process, but he had no idea that Josey's father was also killed. Uncertainties grew wider when Madame K demanded Josey be advanced via a rigged mission, despite failing her original final exam. Ollie's doubts fully subsided when he found out about Dr. Greenburg. He couldn't fathom what big secret could be lurking about Josey and Madame K that would potentially upend everything AWT had built. What could be so bad that it would be worth all this hassle?

After speaking with Josey, Ollie had a bad feeling, an elusive gnawing in the back of his mind that Josey was in imminent danger. He could think of only person to call that might be able to give him an assist.

"I need a favor, kind of a big one," Ollie starts off the phone conversation.

"How big?"

"One hundred K big."

"I'm listening."

"I need you to contact Marty, find out exactly where the team is at right now, and go there immediately."

"Wow. That's a first. What's the trouble?"

"Not sure exactly, just have a funny feeling about Josey's safety. I want you close, but at a distance, you know what I mean. Keep your eyes open. If you get a sense anyone is on to them, you do what you do best. In the event of an actual intervention on your part, they'll be mission money in it for ya. Can you do it?"

"This is highly unusual. You banging her or something?"

"Cute. I'll owe you one. Yes or no? Time is not on our side here."

The man waits for a five count. "Ok."

"Thank you. I'll text Marty and let him know to expect a call. Will you be able to get down there tonight?"

"Where is there?"

"Somewhere in Texas, likely around Houston."

"I should be able to. I'll let you know if there's a problem."

"Good. Be careful out there."

"Will do."

28

Unknown Location

Via Text Message:

"I've sent the location details to you and some other pertinent info. It will happen Friday."

"Good. You'll be handsomely rewarded for your efforts."

"Let's not muddle the truth here. You're making me do this. Everything I've worked for could be gone after this."

"Suddenly you have a spine? Don't let this new-found confidence lead you astray. Remember what's at stake."

"How could I. You won't let me forget."

"Just get it done. If things go south, we'll rendezvous in N.O.L.A., otherwise the usual channels."

29

Mission Day

We've had weeks and weeks to prepare for this mission. Should we succeed, I believe things will settle down for Emily and endless possibilities will open up for us. Should we fail, no matter the reason, I suspect it will be our final mission. Whether some of us will continue on at AWT remains to be seen. For me, personally, I'm under the escalating suspicion that unless there is a big change at the company, I'll soon be running or dead. I don't want to run. Even less, I don't want to be dead. I can't see how this is going to end well for me, either way. There are times when I wish I could go back to a point in time where I had never joined the Kill Academy, a time when I kicked around guys from the Battle Boys, a time when I could see the Leers anytime I wanted.

Unfortunately, that is not my reality. I am where I am and now I have to deal with it. My life depends on it. I keep thinking that maybe the best thing for me to do when we get back to headquarters is to just sit down with Madame K and have a real conversation with her. Almost everything I've heard about my past and her involvement in it has come from the mouth of someone else. Perhaps it's time to hear her side of the story. I have no idea how forthcoming she would be or if I'd be drawing an even bigger target on my back. Either way, sitting on the precipice of some giant secret is getting to the point of being intolerable.

Our drone coverage and its super-duper spying abilities have made this infiltration possible. Without it, I'm not sure we'd even be able to pursue the kill at the Jackson County location. The White Dragon provided use with bird's eye views of the entire property, the layout of a minor security system (which is really only keypad entry from the exterior doors and one to the basement level via the garage), and helped us determine a few blind spots we can use to get close to the house from an adjacent property.

Our agreed upon opinion of the doorway in the garage is that it is an emergency exit and possibly where they take the women in, and probably hidden from the clientele. Based on Vick's recon, we're confident the basement is where the sex trafficking action takes place. This is great information. Emily and Vick are working well together. They're both good at this shit. I just hope Emily avoids a meltdown and can straighten out her head. She was made for this job. Vick was made for it too. I'm still not sure about myself.

Now for the wildcards. We only know that his event is supposed to take place Friday evening. We have no idea specifically what time. We know there will be men guarding this place, at least at the entrances. We have no clue how many. This is Texas. People have guns, lots and lots of guns. We have to assume that every attendee will have one. We have been instructed to make every effort to minimize, if not avoid, all collateral damage. We doubt that will be possible.

I want to be directly involved on this one. Vick is Point. That means I'll be on the adjacent property, hiding off the road about a half-mile away. Originally, I was supposed to have the mini-van, but we decided to simplify things and get rid of it, being so close to the end and all. I'll be watching with a night vision scope and listening with an earpiece, waiting to get involved if Vick calls for backup, to hightail it out of the area when we succeed, or if things go horribly wrong, to take Point. Emily will be in the big van on the property opposite mine. There isn't much she can do other than send the drone up and keep track of the movement on the ground and in the building. She'll guide Vick as he progresses.

I want to go in that house so bad it actually hurts. I want nothing more than to look some of these fuckers right in the face before I beat the shit out of them. I plan on getting the girls out, I just don't know how that's going to be possible yet. If Vick goes in, takes out the targets, and gets out without drawing any attention, I'll have no choice but to leave without doing anything. Once we're safely away, I'll just call the police, as we agreed, though I'd much rather do it myself. Ultimately, I will do what I feel is necessary, regardless of his lack of approval.

Vick is currently with Emily in the van, awaiting the arrival. The sun sets in about thirty minutes. We expect staff, guards, and Denis Koplen to arrive first, followed by the women, then the clientele, which includes Gus Taggert. Once everyone arrives and they all get settled in, that's when the plan will be set in motion.

I'm alone, sitting on my butt in the tall, dry grass. I have a scope on a tripod and a custom assault rifle, not to mention a plethora of small arms and knives, all strapped and holstered to various parts of my body and my black tactical outfit. I have my hair tied back in a ponytail.

In one of my pockets, I'm carrying a few small smoke bombs I can use as cover or a distraction. Emily handed them to me as they were dropping me off at this location. With Vick still in the van, Emily stepped out with me and put a half-dozen of them in my hand.

"Take these," Emily said. "Smoke bombs. They'll fill a twelve by twelve room with smoke in four seconds and can last up to two minutes. Might come in handy."

"Cool. Thanks. You're just full of surprises." I slid them into the left breast pocket of my jacket.

"Be careful out there," Emily said.

"I will. You too."

"Please don't go into that house and do something stupid. I know how you feel about all this."

"I have no current plans to do that."

Emily smirked. "You go in there, you're going to get yourself killed and put this mission in jeopardy. So please don't."

"I will do my absolute best to avoid that. If we all do our jobs, everything will be fine."

"Even if we all do exactly what we're supposed to do, there are always unknowns," Emily said, her tone full of fear and doubt.

"You're freakin' me out again, Em. We've done the work. I'm confident we'll get this done without any hiccups."

She nodded but her worry lingered.

I reached around and patted her on the back of her right arm, smiled, then turned around and took off running to my recon location.

This is the boring part of our work. The waiting. Every thirty seconds, I peek through the scope. Every few minutes, I report what I've seen, which has been nothing.

Finally, full darkness has taken hold. It's just after nine. The sun went down about forty-five minutes ago, the afterglow a memory. My thoughts keep drifting to home. I've enjoyed the relative freedom that has come along with being on a mission, but there's nothing equal to sleeping in your own bed, using your own toilet, being secure. Out here, the motel beds are hard and lumpy, the bathrooms need remodeling and ten gallons of bleach, and our lives are in constant danger. Being a virtual prisoner in the Kill Team house seems like a great place to be right now. Hopefully, I'll be sleeping in that bed within the week.

I'm about to check the scope again when Vick comes through my earpiece.

"Scissors, we have movement."

"Taking a look now," I say.

Our communications will be limited to vague descriptions and codenames just in case anyone else is listening, which is highly unlikely considering the technology we're using. Should we have a listener, it would be difficult to figure out what we're talking about. That's the goal, anyway.

"Rock, I'm seeing five in the caravan, the biggest backing up to the outhouse." The five I'm referring to are a windowless shuttlebus type of van, three black SUVs, and the Mercedes of Denis Koplen. The outhouse is our codename for the garage.

"Copy that," Vick says.

I stay at my scope and watch a stream of young girls and women come out of the back of the shuttlebus, disappearing into the darkness of the garage. Like we thought, the victims are being brought in through the basement tunnel. There are two men I've never seen escorting them down.

Emily says that from one of the SUVs, two men and one woman exit and go directly into the house through the front door. They had the access code for the deadbolt. Six large men in black suits exit the other two SUVs, clearly the security detail. Denis pops out of his car and has a quick meeting with them before they scatter to their various positions and duties. One of them, carrying a large rifle and a flashlight, takes a tour around the property, not the whole thing, but more like a perimeter of two hundred feet on all sides of the house and all the way down the drive to the street. Another one goes into the house through the front door, the others taking positions outside at each entry - one at the backdoor, one at the front, and two at the garage, which has been left open but is dark inside.

Once done with his property tour, that guard settles in as a second guy at the front door of the house. Denis stands outside smoking a cigarette and chatting with them. After a few minutes, he snuffs out the smoke with his shoe on one of the concrete steps, then he enters the house.

I've watched as much of this as I can through the scope, Vick and Emily via the drone. From my perspective, I can see the back of the house and the backdoor, some of the driveway and the front of the garage, and that's about it. I have no angle to the front of the house.

We say very little as the evening unfolds. At exactly 10:22 p.m., black town cars start rolling in, ultimately seven of them, separated by no more than five minutes. They drop off a total of nine men, including Gus Taggert. The town cars promptly leave.

Vick and Emily watch helplessly on their monitors as the women are paraded into the large room upstairs, the men sitting in the surrounding chairs. They count fourteen women, eight monsters, one guard, three staffers, two handlers of the women, Denis Koplen, and Gus Taggert. Vick will have his work cut out for him getting in undetected and doing the job. He'll have to move fast.

By shortly after eleven p.m., the basement level is buzzing with movement. On the main floor, there is only Denis Koplen sitting in the entry parlor. Gus is upstairs with a woman. All the rest are in the basement, including the guard. I don't see any of this myself and it has me twitching with nerves. I have to trust the communications from the rest of the Kill Team, and I do, but knowing what's going on in that house makes me queasy and I want to put an end to it. Maybe it's better I can't see. I might act out irrationally. Janelle Pescaglia comes to mind and how pissed off she was that I let James Orwell get so far in his attempt to kidnap and rape her, probably kill her eventually if I hadn't intervened. I like to think of myself as a person who can evolve, learn, and I sure as shit don't like making the same mistakes over and over again. This is different, or at least I keep telling myself. I'm part of a team now. I have to be reliable. I can't always do what I want. There's no I in T.E.A.M. Yuck. Listen to me. When did I become so corporate? Barf.

"Scissors, the White Dragon has been repowered and I'm ready to engage the scene. Going to start by getting close, around the outhouse and to the back of the pit."

"Copy that, Rock," I say.

"I'm on the move. Paper, let me know if Target Number Two moves."

172

"Copy that," Emily responds.

The house is the pit and Vick is headed to the backdoor for entry. I'll see him perfectly when he reaches the area. Target Number Two is Denis. If all goes to plan, Gus will get it first, followed by Denis. Crossing my fingers for a perfect execution of the plan and the targets.

Ten minutes later, Vick says, "I'm at the back corner of the pit."

"I see you, Rock," I say. There's a small, rickety wooden back porch about five feet wide with six steps up to the door. The guard is sitting on the top step, looking down at his phone. What a shocker. I relay this information to Vick.

"Paper, you got eyes on Target Number Two?" Vick asks.

"Yes. He's coming out of the bathroom on the main floor. He's walking to the front door. He's exited the pit and lit up a smoke."

"Copy that," Vick says. "Unless I say need assistance or until you hear from me, we're on radio silence. Acknowledge."

Emily and I both respond in the affirmative.

And now, Emily and I watch and wait as Vick handles the most difficult part of the job.

30

VICK (Rock)

The heat is making Vick's black tactical outfit difficult to tolerate but he's disciplined enough to not let it bother him. A lesser man would cave. He spent some of his military time in Afghanistan and a short stint in Iraq, so he's a brother to the scorch. Despite the fact this Texas weather is more tropical than arid desert, Vick is well-trained and focused.

He peeks around the corner. There is a dim porch light, orange, near the backdoor, shining a dome of visibility that does not extend past the stairway.

The guard is sitting on the top step, turned sideways, leaning against the post and facing the corner where Vick is hiding in the shadows. The man barely looks up from his phone, fully engaged in a mobile game involving war and trolls.

With a few deep breaths and a quick prayer to the gods of murder and mayhem, Vick hits the safety on his silencer-equipped pistol and emerges slowly from around the corner. He takes immediate action.

Vick is fifteen feet from the guard. He fires one shot to the man's abdomen, shattering his phone. The man has no idea what hit him. He places his hands over the wound, blood spilling between the fingers. A second shot pops and delivers right into the man's forehead, killing him instantly. His head jerks back before falling forward and sending his body down to the base of the steps.

Vick circles around the body and pulls it into the bushes nearby. He ascends the steps, holsters his gun, and removes a tiny spray can from his left leg cargo thigh pocket. He gives it a few shakes then sprays the deadbolt keypad. A clear liquid covers the lock and quickly turns white and icy. After taking his gun back out of the holster, Vick smashes the lock clean from the door using the butt.

He looks through the hole and sees no one, so he pulls the door open, gun out in front of him. He scans the dining room and kitchen quickly. Empty.

Wasting no time, Vick moves to the large viewing room. If someone comes through the front door, the whole mission will turn sour, so he hugs the left wall and takes the stairway, two steps at a time.

The door to Taggert's room is closed. Vick hopes it is unlocked. He turns the knob as slow as he can. After three-quarters of a revolution, he pushed inward, waiting for creaks that never come. A quick look around the room reveals the bathroom door is closed but Vick can hear the shower running, and Gus Taggert is standing at the drink cart, pouring two glasses of an amber-colored liquor.

Gus turns from the cart, one drink in each hand. He freezes at the sight of Vick standing in the doorway, a gun pointed.

Vick takes a gentle step in and closes the door behind him with his free hand.

"The girl in the bathroom?" Vick asks.

Gus nods. "Who the hell are you?"

"I'm nobody. Put the glasses down, slowly, and go over to the bed."

Gus does as instructed with the glasses but doesn't turn around immediately. "Do you have any idea who I am? You're making a big mistake?"

"Shut the fuck up."

"Whatever they're paying you, I'll double it."

"And what about all those girls? You gonna pay them too?"

Gus turns around to face Vick. "Is that what this is all about?"

"I said shut up and get on the bed."

"How dare you boy. I've shat out bigger men than you. I have..."

Vick pulls the trigger. A bullet whizzes across the room and into Gus' stomach.

Gus stands confused. The bullet exited his back and lodged itself into the wall above the drink cart. He looks down to his belly and watches the red circle expand. He wants to speak but chokes instead. He spits blood. It dribbles down his chin.

Vick debates firing a second shot, something he almost always does to ensure death. Instead, he watches Gus stumble sideways, then crumble to the floor.

Vick goes to one of the nightstands after spotting Gus' cellphone. He swipes the screen, brings up the contacts list, finds Denis' number, and hits the text button.

Gus: I NEED YOU UPSTAIRS. GIRL BEING A HASSLE.
Denis: EVERYTHING OKAY?
Gus: I NEED A FAVOR. HURRY.
Denis: ON MY WAY.

The shower is still running. Vick decides not to bother with the girl yet. He moves to behind the bedroom door and waits for Denis. There are footsteps on the stairs, then a light knock.

Vick covers his mouth. "Come."

Denis pushes open the door to find a gun silencer pressed to his temple.

"Shut the door," Vick commands.

Denis takes a step forward and complies. "What is this?"

"A reckoning."

Denis finally sees the body of Gus but doesn't react. "So, you're here to kill us?"

"Something like that. Go over to Gus."

Denis takes a few steps.

Vick pulls the gun away and backs up, still pointing at Denis' head.

Denis stops halfway to the body and asks, "Is there any way this can be resolved, some scenario that doesn't end up with me dead?"

Feeling the crunch of time and tiring of the chitchat, Vick marches toward Denis, puts the gun back to his temple and fires, sending blood, bone, and brain matter across the room and onto the wall and nightstand. The body falls lifeless to the floor, eight feet from his dead boss.

The contract has been fulfilled. Now all Vick has to do is get out and get back to the van.

He doesn't hear the door open and the person step into the room. He does feel the knife enter his back, piercing his spinal cord. He turns his head to face the perpetrator just in time to collapse to the floor. He doesn't feel anything after that.

31

EMILY (Paper)

She watches Vick take off into the darkness, her stomach churning with nerves. The monitor on the remote control shows Vick make his way to the property, behind the garage, and around to the back edge of the house.

Emily thinks constantly about the women in the basement and what they're going through. She knows it's best if Josey does nothing to interfere with the mission, she only wishes the circumstances were different. The faces of her parents enter her mind and she wonders what they would think of the life she now leads, the bad choices she's made, the terrible predicament she's in. They're clueless to her way of life. She hasn't been home to see them for three years but she often longs for reconciliation. The two annual birthday calls she makes are short and awkward.

Emily's eyes are locked on the monitor. She keeps the drone directly over the house while watching Vick execute the guard at the back door and bust the lock. Her pulse races as Vick goes upstairs and kills Gus Taggert. She momentarily loses her breath when she notices the heat signature of Gus cool ever so slightly to a lighter orange.

She turns her attention to the bright spot known as Denis Koplen. He's been outside smoking. Suddenly, he turns to the house, moves toward the front door, and after holding still for ten seconds, steps inside, shutting the front door behind him.

"Shit, shit, shit. He's heading upstairs."

32

JOSEY (Scissors)

I'm suddenly all jacked up with energy. This happens to me right at the beginning of the execution part of each mission, whether I'm Point or Secondary. It's like all the adrenaline my body can produce pushes to the surface. For ten minutes, I'm ready to bust out of my own skin. I always settle down but I definitely have to be careful during that cooling off period.

At this point, my right eye is fixed to the scope. It takes a few minutes, but eventually Vick comes into view as he reaches the back corner of the house. I feel bad for him. I'm just sitting here in basically the same tactical outfit. With all that movement through the darkness, he must be soaked. I do have the advantage of my moisture wicking undergarments, but they are not helping one bit in my efforts to stay dry.

I've been anticipating the observation aspect of this mission. Vick is no nonsense, practical, a dead shot, and as efficient in his movements as anyone I've ever seen. Despite our bickering, I respect the shit out of his game as Point. It's often like a perfectly choreographed dance routine and a marvel to watch.

I see the guard sitting on the porch at the top of the stairs, messing on his damn phone, and quite frankly, doing a piss poor job of being a guard. Little does he know, he's about to become our first collateral damage.

Vick is on the move. Like a cobra, he's on top of the mongoose in seconds, plugging him twice. We're well-trained in close contact firearms. The best and easiest way to take down a target at close range, (and by close range I mean between ten and thirty feet), is start with a shot to the abdomen, then finish them off with a headshot. The first shot staggers the target and slows them down enough to get a more accurate second shot, one sure to kill. It's effective.

The lifeless guard slumps down to the base of the steps. Vick quickly grabs the body under the arms and drags it away into some brush near the foundation of the house. After that, he's right up the stairs. He sprays the lock to freeze it, then busts it with the butt of his gun.

He enters the back door, closing it behind him. Now I have to sit and wait for Vick to report in. I don't expect this to take much time. In order to minimize collateral damage, he needs to get in and out of there in five minutes or less.

I check my dummy phone frequently to see how much time has passed.

Thirty seconds. Too soon.

. . .

Two minutes. Stop checking, Josey. It's been like a minute.

. . .

Three and a half minutes. I'm sure everything is fine.

. . .

Five minutes. Okay, Vick. Time to wrap this shit up.

. . .

Almost seven minutes. He's got this. Stop worrying.

. . .

Nine minutes. Goddamn it, Vick. Come on.

. . .

Ten minutes. Fuck it. I'm making contact.

"Paper, I can't see shit back here. How's everything

looking on our end?"

I count to ten.

"Paper? You getting this? Copy."

I count to five. Shit.

"Rock, I can't get ahold of Paper. How's it going? Copy."

I count to five.

"Rock, if you're listening but can't speak, can you at least give me some kind of static feedback?"

I count to ten.

"Fuck!" I put my eye back to the scope but can't see anything new happening. "What do I do, what do I do?"

Do I charge in? Could just be a communication device issue. Lots of reasons why communications could be down. But the time. It's been too long. Something could be wrong. Maybe Emily was discovered. Maybe Vick too. If I sprint, I can be at the house in two minutes. Fuck it. I'm going.

I knock the scope over, pull a pistol from my hip holster, and take off toward the house.

I make it quickly to the back door. I squat and look through the hole in the door where the deadbolt once was. I don't see anyone.

I enter, pull the door closed behind me, and make abrupt moves with my gun as I scan the rooms in front of me. The house is quiet. Not sure how to take that. Vick's original plan was to go upstairs and take out Gus, call Denis up, then take care of him. If something went wrong, that'd be the place to check first.

I prowl past the kitchen and dining room, through the large room with all the chairs, and take the stairs up. I turn and check behind me every three steps.

At the top, I see the door to the room we assumed was built special for Gus. The door is half open. Maybe Vick got out of there and is on his way back to the van. If so, it's not good that I'm in here. I may be endangering this entire mission, not to mention my own life.

I slide through the open space of the doorway and scan the room. There's no one to the right. The bed is empty. As I turn to the left, confusion takes hold of my mind and I can't seem to process what I'm seeing.

Standing with her back to me is Emily. She has a knife in her hand. I shuffle a step toward the bathroom door. As Emily turns to face me, I see a body on the ground at her feet with a bloody wound in the back. It's Vick. A few feet past Vick is the body of Denis Koplen. Just past him near the booze cart is the body of Gus Taggert.

"What the fuck is going on?" I ask, but I don't know if I really want an answer. I can't think of one that will make sense.

"Damn it, Josey," Emily says, shaking her head. "You weren't supposed to come in here."

"What the hell happened? Why are you in here?"

Emily points the knife at me. I would have laughed if not for the seriousness of the situation. I raise my gun to counter and give her a dubious look.

"I know this must look strange but please give me a chance to explain."

"Strange? Strange? Did you fuckin' stab Vick?"

Tears start to stream from her left eye, then from both. She shakes her head. "I had no choice. They would've killed them if I didn't."

"What the hell are you talking about? Kill who? And put the fuckin' knife down." I wave the gun again as a reminder she's outmatched.

She doesn't comply. "My parents. They got to me during that break after graduating. They blackmailed me. I had no choice. I'm sorry."

"Ahhh ... fuck, Emily!" I start to piece together her words. "Is Vick dead?" My eyes are getting teary. I halt that shit, letting a huge dose of internal rage boil up. I use my free hand to wipe the moisture from my eyes.

"I had no choice. They were gonna kill my parents."

I'm so pissed off I can barely contain myself. I tilt my head back and scream, "Fuuuuuuuuuuuuuck! Why didn't you come to us? We could have helped. The organization could have helped."

"I couldn't risk it. I'm sorry, Josey. I'm so sorry."

"Who did this and what was the goal here? And don't you lie to me or I'll shoot you in the fuckin' face."

"The Kokinos. Their sister died during that F.B.I. raid that Vick was part of. They blamed him ... and Denis and Gus."

I cover my mouth to contain the wrath wanting to escape. The ramifications of this contract are becoming clear to me. The Kokinos got to Emily and paid for a contract to reconcile all kinds of revenge for the death of their sister. This explains why Emily hasn't been herself, especially since the mission details came through. For the second time in my short stint with AWT, I have participated in a rigged mission. What a crock of shit.

"This is unforgivable, Emily. Vick was our partner. We trusted you." Her earlier words about letting down your guard come to mind. What other clues did I miss?

"You weren't supposed to come in here. It was supposed to look like they caught Vick and killed him."

"I can't believe you actually thought you'd get away with this. Now, I'm asking you one last time. Put the knife down."

Emily is full-out crying by now. "I'm ... so ... sorry. I didn't want this," she weeps.

I'm too angry to process her sorrow, too angry to care.

"Please. Just let me leave. You can say I died. You'll never see me again." She drops her arm down, the one holding the knife.

I lower my arm too. I wave her to me. We both take a step toward one another. I sense the knife come up but I'm faster. My gun comes up and I fire twice in quick succession. The knife hits the floor.

Emily gasps. Her eyes apologize again but my heart has no more room. Her hands go to her stomach. Four seconds later, she stumbles forward as I move aside.

The thud reminds me there are other people in this house that could have heard it. I'm in danger. If anyone comes, they'll kill me. I need to leave but part of me doesn't give a shit. I don't know that I care to go on. I can't bear to look at Emily or Vick. My mind goes blank. The minutes begin to fade into nothingness. I collapse to my knees. Like a dam busting wide open, the tears flow. I lean to the left and rest on the footboard of the bed. I'm so tired, so tired. I close my eyes.

33

After being contacted by Ollie, he made quick work to get on a plane and head to Houston. From there, he met with a few men he knows that helped him get the necessary equipment he might require for varying objectives. Within three hours, he had a black Lincoln town car, an arsenal of weapons and ammo, tactical gear, several burner phones, and an assumed identity, all paid for with cash.

Marty had given him enough information to track down the Kill Team. He wasn't there to intervene. His presence was meant to be a shadow, to keep an eye on any potential extracurricular interference that might be swirling, specifically around Josey, and all of this a favor to Ollie.

This kind of operation is not something AWT would normally partake in, nor generally condone. He knows that, but ultimately, he understands, as do Ollie and Marty, that the company does have an interest in protecting its assets, so they're okay riding that fine line. Besides, no one else knows he's involved.

The man hovered around the team as they did their work, unbeknownst to them. He tailed them as they tailed Denis Koplen for that trip down to Jackson County. In disguise, he sat three tables away at the BBQ restaurant and listened to their discussions of the mission and the heart-to-heart between Emily and Josey. From a safe distance, he watched as the team did a test run Wednesday night of the drone and as Vick did a recon loop to the property and through the building. And when it was decided the mission was a go for Friday night, he found a good place of his own to keep an eye on things.

His thoughts kept going back to that overheard conversation between Emily and Josey at the restaurant. Their words kept crawling around in his head like itchy skin under a cast. What he heard gave him pause. Something didn't feel right. Emily didn't seem right. He got the sense Josey could feel there was a puzzle that needed to be solved but she didn't have enough pieces. The man had none of the pieces, just a feeling. His instincts rarely betrayed, however, so he took it seriously.

Marty gave him enough intel to hack their communication systems, a one-way situation. He could hear them but he had no way to talk to them, and it was undetectable. He had positioned himself just a few hundred feet from Emily and the van.

Through night-vision goggles, the masked man has eyes on Emily as Vick leaves the van and the team goes on communication lockdown. It's quiet for a while. Everything appears normal. Vick stays silent. No S.O.S. calls, no hint of trouble. Then Emily puts the drone controller back in the van and disappears into the darkness, heading toward the house.

This behavior confounds the man. He decides to take a chance and goes to the van, fully armed and ready for battle. He pokes around for a few minutes to see if he can figure out what might be happening that would send Emily into the line of fire. The company issued laptop reveals nothing of interest, so he searches the area and finds a bag with another laptop. He boots it up but is disappointed to find it password protected, and not just with the standard operating system login. There is a custom encrypted one in place that he'd have no chance of breaking in the spur of the moment. He turns it off and puts it back where he found it.

As the minutes tick by, the man is aware of the danger of hanging around. Emily, Vick, or both of them could return at any moment, so he hops out of the van. As he starts to walk away and return to his original location, a voice emerges in his earpiece. It's Josey. She's breaking the silence command issued by Vick. No one answers her, perhaps out of protocol. She tries again and again to get through. Nothing. Josey is unaware that Emily has left the van. Suddenly, the masked man is uneasy about the current state of the Kill Team mission. He has a choice to make. He's only there to protect Josey. But he's also a company man. If the mission is going south and he can help fix it, the uppers will likely be happy about that. He decides to make a call.

"Hey, it's me. We have a potential problem."

"What is it?" Ollie asks.

"The team mission seemed to be going fine but something may have happened. I don't know what yet. Tech left the van and I don't know yet to where. Secondary can't get through to anyone on corms. I have a bad feeling. What you want me to do?"

"Shit! Can you get close to the situation and find out what's going on without engaging?"

"Doubtful, but I can try. Let's remember, technically, I have no reason to even be down here."

Ollie lets out a heavy sigh. "Don't worry about AWT. I'll figure something out on that end. I want you to engage. Do whatever you need to. Get our people out if you can. Finish the job if you need to. No witnesses. I'll call in an extraction crew. Once we get our people out, we'll torch the place."

"Okay. I'll let you know when it's done."

"Good."

The masked man gets back in the van and closes the rear doors. He sits in the driver's seat and is happy to discover the keys are still in the ignition. He leaves the headlights off and drives down the road with a gun in his lap. His eyes adjust quickly to the dark. When he reaches the driveway, he pulls the van in and snakes his way toward the house. As he approaches, he rolls down his window. He sees two guards at the garage, two on the front porch of the house. All four are at attention with guns out, instantly on alert when they see the van.

The masked man stops the van at such an angle that he can see all four guards through the side window. He places a hand out of the window and waves over the two guards by the house. They come closer, guns pointed. Before they even realize what is happening, the masked man slides his right arm under his left and fires his gun twice. Each shot lands in the foreheads of the two approaching men. He swiftly opens the van door, slides out of his seat, and using the door for cover, fires four shots at the men guarding the garage. They manage to fire off five shots between them. The van door rattles. The noise stops. The man pokes his head around the side of the door to find both guards dead on the ground. They each have two wounds in the chest.

The man leaves the cover of the door and hurries to the garage guards. Just in case, he puts a bullet into their heads and moves to the garage. Inside, he destroys the deadbolt keypad with a shot from his gun and opens the door, and then descends the stairs. He's not worried about being found. He knows he'll likely have to put anyone down that he comes across, so there's no point in being sneaky.

Staying close to left wall, he walks down the concrete tunnel until he gets to another door, this one without a fancy lock. He tries the knob first. It's unlocked. The hall before him is dimly lit. There are six doors on each side and the hallway seems to open up some fifty feet down.

He pushes open the first door on the left, shoots both the man and the woman on the bed. He pops across the hall and repeats this process. After emerging from the second door, he realizes he has drawn the attention of a handful of people from the open area at the end of the hallway. He runs down and kills a small group of men and women before continuing on with the other ten rooms. It takes him less than four minutes to assassinate eleven men and fifteen women.

From the large open room of the basement, he goes up the stairs, slowly opens the door and does a quick sweep of the entry rooms, the kitchen and dining area, and the center gathering space. Before going upstairs, he opens a door next to the staircase to find a man with a gun, likely one of the guards, sitting on the toilet. At that range, the masked man needs only a headshot to end the threat. The blood and brain matter coat a decorative towel hanging above the toilet, the wall too.

He heads to the second floor. Standing at the bedroom door upstairs, the man turns his head and just listens. There are no voices and no activity, save the muffled sound of a shower running. He wonders, is someone cleaning up?

The door is slightly ajar. He decides to peek in. The door to the right that he guesses is to the bathroom is closed. To his left is a scene he can't quite comprehend. If he didn't know any better, he might assume someone else in his rarified profession had been there to do a big job, other than the team, of course.

For safety's sake, the man first heads to the bathroom door, turning the knob and entering with phantom movements. The room is hot and full of steam from the shower running. He can see a disposable razor in the sink that's been broken apart. The actual blade is missing.

He steps to the tub and shower combo. The white shower curtain is fully closed. He can see the outline of someone sitting in the tub. He snaps the curtain open, his gun pointed. He finds a naked woman leaning back, eye closed like she's enjoying a nice, hot bath, although the shower is running and there is no water in the tub. Both her arms are down at her sides, palms partially open, her arms slit wide open from wrist to elbow. There are flows of blood down her arms, into her hands, and all along her body. The missing razorblade is sitting on the edge of the bathtub.

Back in the bedroom, the man first sees Josey in a sitting position on the floor, slumped over against the foot of the bed. He's disappointed. There is blood everywhere but he can see no obvious wound on her. He steps over and puts two fingers to her neck to check for a pulse.

"Holy shit! Josey? Are you hurt? Josey? Wake up damn it!" With his nondominant left hand, he slaps her across the face.

Her head moves to the right. She opens and closes her eyes repeatedly but otherwise doesn't move.

Figuring if Josey is still alive, others might be too, the man shifts over to Emily to check. She's dead.

"Fuck," he says under this breath.

He steps over Emily's body to Vick's. He can see the blood coming from a small spot on Vick's back. He checks his pulse anyway. It's faint but it's there.

Not giving a shit whether the other two men are dead or alive, he doesn't check their vitals. Based on the gunshot wounds and the amount of blood near each one, he's certain they're dead.

He turns around and pulls a phone from a pants pocket. He dials a number and puts the phone to his head. Josey is coming to and mumbling something he can't quite understand.

"It's me again. How long until help gets here?"

"About an hour," Ollie answers. "Why? What happened?"

"A serious shit-show. The job is done. Point is injured and down. Secondary might be injured but is in shock and otherwise seems okay. Tech Ops is dead."

"Holy fuck! What the hell happened? Who is that I hear?"

"Hang on." The man lowers the phone and looks to Josey. He says to her, "Try to relax and stay calm. We'll be out of here shortly."

"I ... had to," Josey mumbles. "She betrayed us. She ... stabbed ... Vick. I ... had to."

"Who betrayed you, Josey?" The man steps over to her, kneels down in front of her, then removes his mask to reveal himself. "Josey, I'm here to help. Look at me."

She does. She smiles a little when she sees the face of Amatto in front of her.

"Who betrayed you?"

She points to Emily.

"She stabbed Vick?"

Josey nods.

"Vick's alive but needs medical attention. Did you kill Emily?"

Josey's bottom lip quivers as she nods. Tears flow from her eyes as she closes them.

"I'm really sorry about that, Josey. People are coming to get you guys out of here. Vick is going to be okay." Amatto doesn't actually feel confident in those words. "You're going to be okay too. Hold tight."

Amatto rises from his knee and gets back on the phone. "It's Secondary. She says Tech Ops betrayed them, stabbed Point for some reason. Secondary killed Tech."

"I wonder if this hacking issue we've seen has anything to do with this?"

"Hacking issue?"

"Yeah. Someone may have hacked into AWT. Marty is working on it. How's Point?"

"Not sure. He got stabbed in the back, literally and figuratively. He's unresponsive but alive."

"Can you get them out and into the van?"

"I can try."

"Do it, then hang tight. Help will be there soon. And be careful."

"Will do."

Somehow, Amatto gets Josey on her feet, walks her downstairs, and out into the van. He puts her in the front passenger seat.

"I need to go get Vick and bring him down. Sit tight. An extraction crew is on the way. If anyone but them shows up, just keep your head down."

"I left my scope in the field to the west."

"I'll let them know. I gotta go." He turns to exit the van but is stopped when Josey grabs his arm.

"Thank you."

Amatto nods.

He returns to the upstairs bedroom with a collapsible hand truck and two rolls of duct tape. With brute force, he manages to get Vick flat on the hand truck, using the duct tape to secure him.

Like he's hauling a refrigerator, Amatto pushes Vick out of the house and into the back of the van. For Vick's own safety, Amatto leaves him strapped to the makeshift gurney. There may be a serious back injury. Amatto only hopes he hasn't done further damage.

Despite the fact she may have betrayed the team and the company, Amatto decides to retrieve Emily's body too. He takes no such care in getting her to the van. He takes her body by the feet and drags her down the stairs and out of the house, leaving the body on the ground near the van. He'll let the incoming crew handle her from there.

Amatto stays outside near the driver's side door to keep an eye on his surroundings. After twenty minutes, two black conversion vans come down the drive. The lead one flashes its headlights six times to alert Amatto to their presence and as an identifier.

A total of five men and one woman exit the vans. Amatto fills them in on everything he knows happened and what needs to be done. He stands guard as they go to work. One of the men and the woman are medically trained and immediately go to work on Vick. They remove all the duct tape and eventually transfer him to a proper spine supporting gurney, taking him to the back of the first van. After some time, the female medic comes around to Josey, who is sitting in a stupor, looking straight ahead, her mind wandering to places she'd rather not go.

"Josey. Have you been physically harmed in any way?"

Josey snaps from the depths of her mind and shakes her

head.

"Good. If you can walk, I'd like you to come with me to the transport. We're going to take you and Vick out of here. Can you do that for me?"

Josey nods.

The medic opens the door and helps Josey out of the van. With a hand on her elbow, the medic walks Josey to the rear of the first van, assists her into the back, and sits her next to Vick. The other medic is on the other side of Vick, checking the monitor and making notes.

"We're going to leave here in about five minutes. I'll be back in a sec." The woman leaves.

She runs over to Amatto. "We need to get Vick out of here and put him on a jet back home. We'll take her too. She's in deep shock but seems okay otherwise."

"Good. I'll coordinate with the others and get this wrapped up. Someone will have to take this van because I have a vehicle of my own in a field over there." He points east.

"All right then." The medic returns to the transport, hopping into the driver's seat. The vehicle vanishes into the darkness.

In the transport, Josey envelopes Vick's right hand with her own. She still can't wrap her head around the events of the evening. Instead, she chooses to focus on her teammate and the prospect of being home in a bed she knows and back to a life she knows, but one she doesn't really understand.

Ten minutes later, three of the cleanup crew get into the second black van and one of them joins Amatto in the Kill Team van. The crew have planted a few weapons, spread gasoline everywhere, and set the house, the tunnel, and the garage ablaze.

They drop Amatto off at his vehicle and are all on the road in a matter of minutes to catch private jets out of Texas and back to New York.

Behind them are multiple infernos and minor explosions,

soon to attract attention. By the time any authorities arrive, they'll be long gone.

34

Total darkness.
A whirring noise in the distance.
The heat is oppressive.

I take measured steps through the brush. The sound distracts me. I need to concentrate. One misstep and I could break my ankle.

There's a pinch in my left side. I reach down to touch it. There is moisture at my thigh. I bring my hand to my face but can't tell what I'm looking at.

A glint.
The noise is closer.
Much closer.

My leg stings. I want to stop but I can't. I keep moving. Not sure where I'm going. I just keep following the light and the sound. I'll know what to do when I get there. I hope.

The light is flashing now, steady, like a pulse.
The hum is much the same. A moth's wings in slow motion.
The distance closes by half.

There's a bite at my arm. More painful. I wince but keep

moving. I suddenly feel disoriented. I stop and turn to the right. The light is still there. I turn around. The light is there too. The sound is getting closer. I feel my body temperature rise. My heart races. I feel a presence. It's Vick. He standing right in front of me. Something shiny and sharp emerges from the black. I want to scream but can't. I reach out. He collapses and disappears into the night. I hear a whisper. I turn around.

The light has turned from white to orange.
The sound is overhead. Louder. A drone, although, too big.
The air has turned too thick to breathe.

Emily. She's holding a knife. I wipe the sweat from my forehead. It stings my eyes. I try to speak but the words get caught in my throat. The noise is deafening. I place my hands over my ears and close my eyes. I have a sharp pain in my stomach. I open my eyes. Emily is gone. What light there is has turned red. My eyes drift down. Blood is rushing from a wound in my abdomen. There is a jolt of lightening in my back. I fall to my knees and crumble to the ground. Emily. I trusted you. How could you do this to us?

35

Sunday Morning

I wake from a restless night of vivid nightmares, drenched in sweat and catching my breath. There's a bottle of water on the nightstand next to the bed. I have no idea where it came from. I do recognize the room I'm in as the dorm I lived in during my training at the Kill Academy. I sit up in bed and grab the water, taking a few long drinks. The alarm clock reads: 8:13 a.m. I check my wristwatch and it says 7:13, but also lets me know it's Sunday. I have no recollection of yesterday. Friday, well ... I'm already trying hard to forget.

I still can't seem to wrap my head around it. There's a pressure on my chest yet it feels like it's years and miles away, almost like someone had told me this terrible story about death and betrayal and failure that happened to someone else. I know the reality of it. My head and heart tell me I was there. It's suddenly difficult not to question every choice I've ever made.

I want a hot shower, an Irish coffee, and a boat to sail away toward the horizon, never once looking back. Currently, I will have to settle for the shower and a coffee with half and half.

I find my bags of clothes and other personal belongings at the end of the bed. I wonder if they went through them. I hope not. I have burner phones the company doesn't know about and ten times as much cash in there then is normal for being on a mission. I find a clean pair of black cargo pants, a black tank-top, underwear, and socks.

Hitting the showers here brings back memories of my training. Part of me hopes that when I go to the cafeteria to get coffee I will find that the last year was just a dream and I'm back at our original tour of the Kill Academy. That way, when the day is done, I can walk away from this place and never look back. I could go and visit the Leer family, have a pizza with them, and drink some cheap scotch before falling soundly asleep on the S.S. Mine Now. Unfortunately, that is not my life anymore, and it hurts like a son of a bitch.

The halls are quiet and the cafeteria empty. I stare at a blueberry muffin for thirty seconds before deciding I had better just stick to coffee for now. I sit at the table furthest from the door and facing it. Half my coffee is gone in the blink of an eye.

My mind drifts to Vick. I have no idea where he is. I know the company has a private, off-site medical facility. When we get shot or something, obviously, we can't just go to the hospital. Based on what I overheard from the medic on the jet, Vick will need surgery, but just how serious his injuries are is beyond me. I remember hearing the word paralysis. I need to see him. I need to talk to him. I need him to be okay.

Dina and the Dean walk through the door and come over to my table. I know what's coming and I don't want it to.

"Glad to see you're up and about," Dina says. "How are you feeling?"

"Been a rough couple of days. How's Vick?"

"He's alive and in recovery. He's been in and out of consciousness. Still a wait and see situation." Dina is trying hard to keep her body language from revealing too much. That's not a good sign.

"We really need to discuss the mission," the Dean says.

"I know it won't be easy," Dina says, "especially so soon, but it's critical we get some information from you. We'd like you to at least try and see how it goes."

"I don't know if I'm ready."

"There could be lives at stake," Dina rebuts. "There are things that happened that you might not know about."

"Like what?"

"Come talk to us and we'll fill you in."

I concede with a nod and rise from the table. I walk over and they let me pass.

"We'll go to my office," Dina says.

When we reach the door to Dina's office, she uses her fob to gain entry, then she takes a seat behind her desk. The Dean and I take the only two other seats in front of the desk, me in first, then the Dean, effectively pinning me in. It makes me uncomfortable. The last thing I need to feel right now is trapped.

"So, let's just start with the basics," the Dean says. "Up until Friday, how did mission prep and recon go?"

I think back on all the time we spent in Texas. Other than Emily's erratic behavior, which in hindsight should have been a giant fucking red flag of a warning, all the planning went well. Of course, there was the little incident where I had a knife to my throat while on Denis recon, but there's no way in hell I'm saying anything about that.

"For the most part, everything came together as good as could be expected. Emily had been highly emotional at times, something that did worry Vick and I, but she had been acting that way since well before the mission, so we had no reason to believe it had anything to do with it."

The Dean and Dina look to one another like I just revealed something they already knew.

"What?" I ask, glancing to each of them.

"It has been discovered that someone hacked into AWT," Dina says, "poking and prodding for months trying to get into the databases. Tisha and Marty have uncovered some very disturbing things on Emily's equipment. It's still uncertain exactly what she was looking for and what she may have seen."

I rub my head. "Of course. That makes so much sense now."

"What does?" the Dean asks.

"Why Emily was acting so weird for months." I take a deep breath. The time has come for me to face what happened in that room Friday night. I don't want to open that door. I'm terrified to see what's really there.

"Right before I shot Emily," the words stick hard in the back of my throat, "she told me someone had gotten to her right after we graduated. They must have blackmailed her. She said they threatened to kill her parents if she didn't cooperate."

"Jesus!" Dina says.

"Yeah. She said the Kokinos wanted Vick, Gus Taggert, and Denis Koplen dead. They blamed their sister's death on them."

"Vick? Why Vick?" the Dean asks.

"He was part of some snafu when he was with the F.B.I. Something down in Texas. Apparently, their sister was killed. They must have tracked Vick down and found out about him being here. They chose Emily, likely because she could get access to AWT in ways others like Vick or myself couldn't."

"And you're absolutely sure about this?" Dina asks.

"Positive. I don't see why she would have lied at that point."

The Dean jumps from her chair like someone set it on fire. She looks to Dina, who nods and waves her on, then she runs from the room.

"Amatto said you told him, that after Vick killed Gus and Denis, Emily stabbed Vick, then you showed up and killed Emily. Is that how it went down?"

"Best as I can tell. Can I ask you something?"

"Go ahead."

"Where is Ollie?"

"He's offsite. Hasn't left Vick's side since you guys returned."

More evidence of the character of Ollie. I know he wanted

to talk to me about something when I got back. It sounded serious. I can't help but wonder.

"I need to see Vick."

"Soon. Right now, you can imagine that things are kind of tense around here. But soon. Once Madame K releases the hold, we'll make sure you get over there to see him."

"Hold?"

"AWT is basically on personnel and communication lockdown until we figure out exactly what happened and how vulnerable we might be. Certainly, you can understand the danger we all might be in?"

"I suppose."

"Do you really need to suppose?"

"No."

"Up until about three minutes ago, we had no idea Emily might have been blackmailed by the Kokinos. That will accelerate this process."

It dawns on me how AWT might treat people like the Kokinos after being betrayed by them. I cringe.

Just to be a pest, I decide to ask. "So, what will happen to them?"

Dina raises her eyebrows, tilts her head, confirming my thoughts.

"I can imagine they're in the wind now."

"Not for long."

"I find this whole thing weird. Did they actually think they were going to get away with this?"

"I don't know."

I ponder what Emily said to me. She said I wasn't supposed to be in there. "I don't think Emily was expecting me to engage as quickly as I did. My guess, she was hoping to kill Vick, get out of there, and let the whole thing look like he was killed in action. We'd be none the wiser."

"That makes sense. And in that case, the Kokinos and Emily could have pulled this whole thing off."

"Exactly. Scary how close they were."

"Your efforts may have saved lives around here." Dina

leans back in her chair, pausing for a moment to take it all in.

"I'm really tired all of a sudden. Any chance we can pick this up later?"

"Of course. Thank you, Josey, for everything. Come talk to me whenever you need to. I know this must be hard. What you had to do." She shakes her head. "Go ahead and get some rest. Eat if you can."

"Okay."

I stand and scoot past the chairs. Dina is immediately on her phone. I leave the office.

Walking back to my room, I realize I need to pee, so I head to the bathroom first.

After using the toilet, I wash my hands, then look into the mirror. For a split second, I see Emily's face and not my own. I look away and then back again. My reflection stares back at me. I notice the dark circles under my eyes for the first time.

Like I'm questioning someone else and demanding answers, I ask, "How are you gonna get through this, Josey? How?"

She has no response. She can't imagine how.

"You had to kill your teammate, your friend."

I shake my head.

"You attract danger. You ever notice how everything you touch turns to shit? You shouldn't be around other people. They might end up dead."

"Fuck you," I answer back. "Fuck you!"

I draw my right arm back and punch the mirror, shattering the glass. It stays in place, my blood in the center and now dripping from my hand into the sink.

I move to the left and turn around, afraid to look again. I fall against the wall and can no longer hold myself up. I slide down to my butt and burst into tears.

36

The Bridge at AWT

There had been an unspoken tension between them for months. For both Tisha and Marty, it was clear they had competing loyalties at AWT, but when it was discovered that one of their own had sabotaged a Kill Team mission and had been attempting for months to hack into the network, servers, and databases of the company, they quickly banded together to ensure full security.

They make a list of likely vulnerabilities and unusual activity, taking turns to double and triple check every possible irregularity, every entry point, every log file.

After five hours, they discover an employee in small munition sales had clicked a link in a suspicious email that turned out to be a phishing email. It sent network and login information to an unknown location hidden by a VPN behind multiple firewalls and encryption. As far as they can tell, no private information was actually stolen, but that was only because the plan had failed. They are still left with the uneasy feeling of not knowing what Emily was looking for.

Despite their confidence that no other data was taken, Tisha and Marty make minor changes to beef up security. They work from their stations on The Bridge.

"You get that login file copied and sent to me?" Tisha

asks.

"Doing it right now," Marty answers, sipping on a bottle of raspberry tea. He rubs his eye. His vision is starting to blur from the nearly nonstop computer work they'd been doing since word had gotten around about Emily and the soiled Kill Team mission.

Tisha has kept a steady stream of mocha Frappuccino's and powdered sugar donut holes at her desk, but even she is starting to feel the power of time. She yawns long and loud.

"So, how long did you know about all this?" Marty asks. His own curiosity has been begging him to probe Tisha into revealing the fact that she's known about the hacking attempts since they started, and that she's been reporting them to Madame K, and only Madame K, all along.

"Huh?"

"You heard me. How long?"

Tisha pretends to puzzle over the question but she knows exactly what Marty is asking. She doesn't know how she wants to answer. At this point, she figures, what difference does it make?

"I picked up on it right away. Well before they went down to Texas. Since we're just laying it all out on the console, how long have you known that I knew?"

"Since well before they went down to Texas, not long after you did."

"I figured as much. Why didn't you say anything?"

"Probably the same reason you didn't. We answer to different people at times."

Tisha ponders the implication. "Well, I answer to the top dog. Anybody else is irrelevant."

"Usually. But things change ya know. Leaders come and go. The sands of time may be turning over around here. Certainly, you've felt it?"

"Hard not to. People chitter around here like sparrows in a bush."

"We make a helluva team, though, you and I. I hope that continues, no matter what lay ahead."

"I couldn't agree more. Now, more than ever, we probably need to stick together. This breach ... this bad juju around here ... people can lose their heads, and I mean that literally."

Marty takes another drink from his tea. "I like my head right where it is, thank you very much."

"Me too," Tisha says. "Meeeee too."

37

Monday

I managed to eat a full lunch today. Beef stir-fry with a couple of egg rolls. Until then, I had only gotten down a few saltine crackers and a strawberry cereal bar, not counting the coffee. There's something about the normality of eating that makes me feel better, like having no appetite is a constant reminder of how sickening the last few days have been.

I've mostly just been sitting around, nerding on the net, reading stupid pop culture shit, trying to find anything to distract from the current situation. There happens to be twenty-four hours in a day and I've only been sleeping in spurts, so that's a lot of damn time to fill.

I wander the halls sometimes too. I thought about hitting the shooting range, but as yet, I can't bring myself to pick up a gun, let alone fire one. The gym caught my eye a few times too but I just don't have the strength or energy. Besides, running in place for an hour just doesn't feel like a good way to exert myself. If I'm going to run, it's going to be away from this place, never to return.

I'm on my way back to my room when I run into Amatto coming from the bathroom.

"Hey. How you holding up?" Amatto asks.

"Going a little stir crazy, to be honest. I really want to go see Vick."

"I know what you mean. I've heard Vick is finally awake. Hopefully, he'll be okay."

I rub my forehead. "I just can't. Uhh, god, how could we be so blind to this? How could I be? I knew something was wrong. I knew it, and yet I didn't do anything. Fuck."

"Don't do that to yourself. Sometimes, we're just too close to a situation to be objective."

"I know you're right, but this ... this is bad."

"I won't lie, it's pretty bad, but the world we run in," Amatto shakes his head, "we're always knee-deep in shit. That's the nature of it."

"I don't know if I want to do this anymore."

"Be careful who you say that to around here. You might get your wish."

"I'm serious though. How do you, personally, stay engaged, yet somehow detached from the reality?"

"I don't. I just accept what I am, what we do, all the nasty shit, all the good shit. It would tear apart even the strongest person if they didn't."

"Maybe I just can't do that. What chance do I have then?"

"No chance at all."

He's right and I know it. This is the kind of work where doubt, minor mistakes, and half-hearted effort and commitment get you killed.

"Thanks for always being truthful with me. I hear ya. I just don't like it."

"Despite my better judgment, I've grown kind of fond of you. You're kind of like the little sister I never had and probably never wanted."

I feel my face turning red. I playfully wave him off. "The feeling is mutual."

"Well, as much as I'd like to keep standing here being all wise and brotherly and shit, I'm on my way to chat with Ollie, so be good. I'm sure we'll see each other again soon."

"He's back?" I blurt, instantly wanting to retract my obvious level of excitement.

He gives me a stare that lets me know he's on to us.

"Tell him to come see when he gets a chance."

"Okay." He walks away.

I stay in place for a moment. Part of me is happy that Ollie is back in the building. There's a certain safety net there for me. But now my head hurts. I don't want to think about this crap anymore. Puppy and kitten videos. That's what I need to distract. I continue on to my dorm, get into bed but sitting up, and with my laptop, disappear into small animal heaven.

38

"How long is this damn lockdown gonna go on?" Amatto asks Ollie. They're sitting in Ollie's office with a device activated that will garble any attempt to record their conversation from outside sources.

"Probably just a few more hours. Madame K wants to talk directly to Josey first, and to the leadership, which is why I'm even here at all. Tech team seems confident we're okay though."

"Good. I'm ready to get the fuck out of here. It's been a long week and I need a liquid distraction."

"Yeah. At this point, we might as well throw a kegger for the whole organization. Anyway, I'll get right to it. I have an assignment for you."

"Oh? New contract come in? Not a moment's rest around here."

"No contract. Disaster recovery. Nestor and Sophia Kokinos. Brother and sister that paid for the Kill Team contract, blackmailed Emily. I need you to find out what information they were trying to get out of our system. Then I need them gone."

"Oh. Clean up, aisle twelve."

"Something like that. Li Xia and I will be working on a dossier with what information we can muster, but you'll have to dig deep on this one. I'm sure they'll have disappeared, laying low for a while. Most likely overseas. Probably be a week or two before we'll be ready, so you can relax for a bit."

"A good start would be getting me outta here tonight. Sleeping in the dorms again like some trainee sucks."

"Agreed. Hang tight. You'll be the first to know when we get the all clear. Before you go, I wanted to ask you about Josey."

"What about her?"

"It seems like you two are real simpatico, if you know what I mean."

"We have a mutual respect and admiration. What's the ask?"

"I have to tell her something, something she's not going to like, and she's probably going to feel like I've been lying to her."

"Have you been lying to her?"

"More like, didn't reveal everything I know about something very personal to her, but I need to tell her now, before she gets too deep into this thing. It will be much worse, for her and me, if she finds out later."

"Does this thing connect to the rigged training mission in Baltimore? Cuz if it does, you better watch your ass. That little ball of spitfire is going to rain down holy hell on you. With all this shit that just happened, you sure this is the best time to do it? Last thing she needs is another asshole liar in her life. She might go nuclear."

"I figured as much, but I don't have a choice. She and I have ... well," Ollie stops short of revealing his real feelings for Josey.

"I knew it!" Amatto shakes his head. "Are you sure it's a good idea to be bangin' your subordinates?"

"I know. There's just something about that woman. Fuck."

"I get it. You're into that kinda damaged chick. She does have a strange magnetism. Might be the deadly kind."

"Trust me, I question my decision every day, but I'm too

far in now to back out."

"You want some advice?"

"Go ahead."

"Be vulnerable. No machismo bullshit. On the outside, she's made of steel, but her heart is always in pieces. If you're going to fracture it more, start to find a way you can stitch it up too. Might take a while, but if you don't, she's never going to respect you again, let alone trust you."

"Since when did you become the Dalai Lama?"

"As soon as you people starting fuckin' things up around here. But I am on a roll today."

Ollie gives Amatto a scowl, then smiles.

"Touché. Alright. Thanks. You can get outta my hair now."

"Good. I need to go shoot something."

39

Over the last few hours, I've managed to center myself and find some perspective on this whole Emily affair. Though it's easier just to blame myself for not interpreting the signs sooner, or blame Emily for not being strong enough to get help from us, or blame Vick for whatever flub occurred at the F.B.I., or blame the company for putting us in that position to begin with, I've accepted the fact that the Kokinos are the only ones at fault here. They unfairly targeted Vick, blackmailed Emily with a threat to her parents, hired us under false pretenses, and ultimately, caused the deaths of nearly thirty people, all in exchange for the pain and loss of one person – their sister Phoebe.

I can only guess what the company will do to them. There is always a lot of talk around here about an imaginary scale, whereby, through the normal channels of justice, the powerful and evil are always ahead. Our services steady the equilibrium. Do two wrongs make a right? I used to think so, especially from my days on the streets of Baltimore, but at this level, I'm not sure anymore.

I try not to think about the innocent lives taken during the cleanup of our mission. Those girls and women did nothing to deserve that. Amatto reminded me of the protocol. I understand the hows and whys but they do nothing to appease my sensibilities. It only works to piss me off more.

Going forward, when my conscience tells me to act, I will, regardless of company fucking policy.

I'm startled by a knock at my door. My instincts send my eyes scrambling around the room in search of anything I wouldn't want others to see, then I remember where I am.

"Come in."

The knob turns, the door swings open, and into my room walks Madame K, alone. I knew we'd be having a private conversation at some point. I did not expect her to come to me. She closes the door.

I jump from the bed. "Madame K."

"Josey." She stays by the door.

I remain close to my bed. It suddenly feels awkward. I can't help but wonder how much she knows about what Ollie and I have been up to. Someone knows. Getting threatened at knifepoint in Texas made that crystal clear.

Seeing her standing before me again, I'm reminded of the power and stature her presence brings to a room. On one hand, she is my boss and I should fear and respect her, but on the other hand, she may have played some part in the death of my parents, in which case, I should fear and despise her. Clearly, I have no idea how to act right now.

"By all accounts, Vick seems to owe his life to you."

"Maybe. Amatto is the one that really swooped in and saved the day."

"Humble. I like that."

"Well, I kind of fell apart there at the end."

"That's understandable. Your mission was tainted and you had been betrayed. Killing her was the right thing to do, though I'm sure it must have been difficult."

A lump develops in my throat. I have no desire to speak so intimately with this woman, not right now, and sure as hell not about Emily. My body language must be telling that story. I can't help but show it.

"With enough time, your nerves will steady. This work hardens us all."

"I don't know if that's actually a good thing. Isn't our

belief in humanity why this work is important and necessary?"

"Yes, yes. You speak to Dina enough, you'll come out on that side of it. But surely you can see, even as inexperienced as you are, that it's never that black and white?"

I nod. She's right and I don't like it one bit. There are a thousand ways to justify this work and an equal number of ways to dismiss it. That battle will rage on forever.

I decide to probe a little. "So, I'm sure you've seen some serious shit in your day?"

She chuckles and smirks. "You don't get to where I am without having done so. There are no clean hands around here, least of all mine."

That was surprisingly forthcoming. Everyone knows her reputation, but it always precedes her. She never has to talk about it. There are plenty of little birdies chirping the stories and legends that are Madame K.

"Keep in mind," she adds, "there will be times when your actions will leave a bad taste in your mouth, though you'll know you did the right thing. It comes with the territory. Many of the things we do, things you'll end up doing, will be terrible yet satisfying. If you can't get used to that, and quickly, your days here are numbered, period."

And the hammer hits. Find a way to cope or get out.

"Well, I have another meeting to attend." She turns and opens the door, takes one step, then turns back around. "I've noticed you have quite the rapport around here, but I would caution you. Be careful with whom you place your trust. Everyone has secrets and motivations. Self-preservation is everyone's greatest priority, even mine, even yours, whether you know it or not."

She doesn't wait for a response. She's gone and the door is shut before I can even react.

I'm uncomfortable, off-center. I can imagine she gets the last word in every conversation she has, and this one no exception. We started off so well, but when you finish with veiled threats and diversions, the complimentary start is lost. I do get the impression she was trying to soften the blow of decisions she may have made in the past, ones that might have affected me directly. I could be digging on that one. Madame K is the last person I can think of that would make excuses, but that's what I'm left with.

40

Madame K's Office

Madame K is in her chair, facing the windows behind her desk. Considering how bad the Kill Team mission turned out and the potential hacker issue, she has remained relatively calm. Everyone knows this façade won't last.

The Dean, Dina, and Ollie are standing on the other side of the guest chairs in Madame K's office, all of them keenly aware that keeping their distance from the boss for this meeting is safer, just in case she starts throwing things. This isn't the first contract breakdown the company has experienced, nor will it be the last, but with the internal power struggles in full display, the tensions and stakes have never been higher.

"I'm just going to start by asking, how the hell did we not see this coming?" Madame K keeps her position looking away from the others. She raises her voice a bit, "I mean, Jesus! With the resources we have around here, this feels like a major fuck up. Give me one good reason why I shouldn't just fire all of you right now."

"Despite the fact there was a mild connection to Vick from his F.B.I. days on this one, we could find no connection to the Kokinos," The Dean says. "We now know that their sister Phoebe was finally identified as one of those killed during that F.B.I. raid, but it had not been documented anywhere until after we accepted the contract."

Madame K leans back in her chair, then spins around to face the trio. "I trust I don't need to remind you how easily this whole organization could come undone. We all must be the best versions of ourselves around here. I feel we might be getting sloppy."

The last part infuriates Ollie, though he doesn't show it. She's made that insinuation before, most of the time landing it firmly on his shoulders. He couldn't disagree with her assessment more.

Madame K goes on, "Perhaps we're not discerning enough with some of these contracts. We must work hard to minimize risk. This business is so dangerous already."

"You mean like the second Josey training mission," Ollie snaps back. He just couldn't help himself.

Dina and the Dean throw glares at Ollie, fully understanding how much gasoline he just threw on the already raging inferno.

With eyes locked on Ollie, Madame K uses her left hand to point to Dina and the Dean. "You two, get out."

"I would encourage all of us to bring the intensity and rhetoric down a notch," Dina pleas. "Nothing good will come of it."

"Dina, if you're still standing in my office ten seconds from now, I can't guarantee your safety. Now, GET OUT!"

The threat sinks deep into Dina's stomach. She's heard the wrath of her boss before but she's never once threatened physical harm. She turns and storms from the room.

The Dean looks to Ollie, shrugs her shoulders, then follows Dina out, shutting the door firmly behind her.

"Why do you constantly feel the need to make me look like a damn fool, Tolliver?"

"Though I doubt anyone around would say it to your face, especially considering you just threatened arguably your most loyal employee, you have become unhinged."

"So, what, you're the appointed spokesperson for this

tiresome rabble?"

"You might scare everyone else, but you don't scare me."

Madame K rises from her chair and slams her hands down on the desk. Ollie doesn't budge. "Maybe you should be. You'd be nothing without my guidance and training. You were sitting behind a fucking desk at the C.I.A. before I plucked you out of there and made you what you are today. I may be older, but I'm as strong as ever, so be very careful here."

"You haven't killed anyone of importance in a decade, unless you count helpless children's home directors."

"You're officially suspended from duties for two weeks."

"Really? This is such bullshit."

"Get out."

"Fine."

Ollie storms out, slamming the door behind him.

Down in his office, after gathering up his things to take home, he plops down in his desk chair, ready to punch a hole in the nearest wall. He doesn't. He contemplates the idea of leaving and never coming back, but he doesn't want to leave people hanging, people he actually cares about. As bad as things have become at AWT, he knows this is only the beginning. The situation will likely get worse, much worse.

He figures that once he leaves the building, his access will be temporarily revoked, so he decides he'll just take Josey to see Vick and use her access to get in, and finally have a talk with her.

41

My stomach churns as another knock at my room comes too soon. I don't want to talk about this goddamned failed mission anymore. I don't want to discuss whose fault it was, the ethical and moral gray areas, or my fucking feelings. Enough already.

"Come."

To my surprise, Ollie walks in. This is the first time I've seen his face since our meetup in Randallstown. Part of me wants to hug him, throw him on the bed, or maybe have him throw me on the bed, but obviously we aren't going to be doing that here.

"Gather up your shit, we're going," Ollie says. "Meet me in the parking deck in five minutes." He doesn't leave any room for hellos or a discussion. Before I can even open my mouth to respond, he's gone, the door shut.

What the hell happened? Are we suddenly in danger? Why the urgency? I don't have time to think about it, so I grab my bags, stuff the few clothing items I have draped over a chair into them, and double check I have my phones and all the money I brought with me from Texas. I'm out of my room, up the elevator, and to the parking deck in just three minutes.

I emerge from the elevator and look around. I see Ollie standing by a black SUV, using his cell phone. I rush over to him.

"Get in. We'll talk on the way."

I pop the rear hatch and throw my bags in. I enter the backseat from the passenger side. Ollie hops in a few seconds later.

The driver pulls out of the parking deck and heads north. He's not Ollie's personal guy, just one of the guys that would transport me or the team to the house. That makes this a little unusual.

"Why did we just rush out of headquarters?"

"We're going to see Vick. I assumed you'd want to."

"Well, yeah, but why the sudden urgency." He still hasn't looked me in the eye. He's hiding something.

"I've been suspended for two weeks. I probably won't be able to get into the building where Vick is unless I piggyback your access."

"Jesus, Ollie. What happened?"

"I pissed off the boss. What else?"

"Must've been pretty bad to get suspended. How serious is it?"

"For now, it's okay. In two weeks, we'll see if I'm allowed to come back."

"Honestly, I don't think I want to go back if you're not there. I wouldn't feel safe."

"I don't think anyone is safe right now. With that thing you and I have been digging through, us most of all. Which reminds me. I have something important I need to talk to you about, after we see Vick though. We need real privacy."

"Okay. How long 'til we get there?"

"We're there now."

"That was quick. I'm nervous, Ollie."

"I know. I got word that he's been awake, which is great news."

I'm trying to relax and focus. "Has he said anything? Like, does he know everything that happened?"

"Nothing of consequence, and no, he doesn't know all the details yet. That's where you and I will come in. You ready for that?"

"Hell no! I'll let you take the lead."

The SUV pulls into a parking space behind a small brick building. We came across a bridge and into Jersey on the way here, but didn't go far.

"That's fine. Let's go."

We exit the vehicle and make our way into the facility.

The interior of the building reminds me of the last dentist's office I went to for a cleaning. Beige carpet, sky blue fabric on the waiting room chairs, brightly lit, receptionist behind a large counter. The main differences are the fact I have to use my fob to get in and there isn't a single person waiting to be seen.

Ollie waves at the receptionist. She waves back, smiles. We head around to the left, through an unsecure door, down a short hallway, and to the last door on the right, labeled – ROOM G.

The room is much like one might see in the intensive care unit of the average hospital. There's a TV mounted high to the left, monitors and others devices on wheels, leather lounge chairs, a bathroom, and in the middle of the wall to the right – Vick sitting up in an expensive looking hospital bed. He smiles when he sees me, which helps to soften my mood and ease my stress.

Vick speaks quietly but enthusiastic, "Josey!"

I rush over to him and hug him gently. "How are you feeling?"

"I think I might be on too many drugs to know." Vick waves to Ollie, who does the same.

I smile. "Ollie has been by your side since you got here, save for the last few hours where he had to go to headquarters for a bit."

"Thank you. I'm still a little fuzzy. They won't tell me anything. What the heck happened?"

"I'll let Ollie tell you." I step back and sit in the chair nearest bed.

Ollie takes a step forward to the end of the bed. "What

can you remember?"

"Not much. The last thing I remember is seeing Gus and Denis on the floor. After that, I have a brief recollection of being on a jet, then waking up here."

My mind wanders and my ears seem to take on a tunnel effect as Ollie fills Vick in on the details of the mission, Emily's betrayal, and the whole messy affair of Amatto bailing us out and getting us back to New York. I look up every once and a while to gauge Vick's reaction to certain things. In most cases, he is befuddled and hurt.

Ollie turns the conversation to Vick's health. I then start to emerge from my cloudy headspace and listen in. I hear the words - severed nerves ... don't know if I'll ever walk again ... months of recovery and physical therapy.

Part of me wants to cry. Part of me wants to murder someone. Part of me wants to crawl in a hole somewhere and never come out. Then I hear my name.

"Josey," Vick says.

I lift my head and make eye contact. "Yeah?"

"You saved my life. If you hadn't charged in and stopped her, I wouldn't be here right now. I owe you a debt that I may never be able to repay."

I try to be funny. "Roger that." Ollie looks at me funny but Vick and I both share a laugh. "Seriously though, we all owe Amatto that debt. If he hadn't showed up, I don't know what. Which begs the question, and perhaps you can shed some light on this, Ollie, but how did Amatto even come to be there?"

Ollie turns to me. "How much does he know about the thing?"

"Pretty much everything," I say.

"Okay, well, after you called me and told me about the Houston incident with the guy with the knife, I got a bad feeling, so I called Amatto and asked him to keep an eye on you for a while, make sure you were safe. He caught on to the strange happenings in Jackson County. He called me and I told him to engage. Then I sent the cleanup crew to get you guys home."

"So, maybe you're the one we should be thanking." I say.

"Yeah," Vick confirms.

"I don't think so. My part was just luck. Amatto did the actual work there. Regardless, I'm just glad you two got out alive."

"Hey, Vick, you don't mind if I steal Josey away for a sec? I need to chat with her real quick."

"Sure. Just come back and see me before you leave."

"I will. We'll be right back."

Ollie turns to me and tilts his head toward the door. I get up and follow him out of the room.

"Let's go outside," Ollie suggests.

We head out the same way we came in and walk to the corner of the building, away from the entrance and the SUV we came in.

"What's up?" I ask.

"I have something I need to tell you and you're not going to like it." Ollie's facial expression is now dire and morose. "But please understand, I'm on your side."

"That's a helluva way to begin. Just spill it."

"I won't bother sugar-coating it. I knew from the second you were recruited that your mother and father were killed by the company via a contract."

"What?" I'm confused. "You knew?"

"Yes, but let me explain. Dina and I both thought it was foolhardy to even recruit you knowing that. If you found out, obviously, it would be a problem."

"Oh, it's a BIG fuckin' problem! I trusted you, Ollie." I'm fuming.

"What we didn't know was you. When you failed the first training mission and Madame K wanted to rig a new mission just to get you graduated, we became suspicious of her motivations. We have never done anything like that at AWT before. There was clearly more to the story of your parents, and of course to you. And we still don't know the full story."

I turn away, unable to look at him. I want to punch him in

his perfectly chiseled jaw. I resist, for now. I can't think of a single word in rebuttal. I am feeling many things. Heartache, disloyalty, anger, and loneliness. Once again, this world I've entrenched myself in has proven to be exactly what I've believed it to be.

"I'm sorry, Josey. I really am. But I'm on your side. You have to believe that."

"I don't have to believe jack-shit, you fucking liar."

"Certainly, you can understand my position here. I have no reason to even be here with you right now. What do I gain from supporting you, helping you? My ass in on the line here too. Hell, we both might end up dead because of this shit."

I hear his words and the truth in them but that doesn't seem to alleviate the pain. I want to be alone.

"I need to go home, gather myself, think about this mess."

I start to walk away, then stop and turn back to Ollie.

"Don't contact me. When I'm ready to deal with you, I'll call you."

I whip back around and jog to the SUV. I hop into the backseat. "I'm ready to go home. Take me to the Team house."

"Is he coming?" the driver asks.

"He's going somewhere else. Now, let's go."

42

The house was quiet when I arrived, lifeless. My kitty is still with Mark the Uber driver and will probably have to stay on the farm there. I have no idea what the coming months are going to entail, so better for her to have a consistent and steady home. I feel terrible for even adopting her. I should have known my lifestyle would get in the way.

I got home around dinner time but had no appetite. I immediately went to my room, slammed the door as hard as I could, and collapsed on the bed, asleep in minutes. I keep having dreams of giant drones and Vick being stabbed. It kills me to think he may never walk again. Our team is decimated. One is dead, one is likely crippled, and one is ready to fly the coup. And fly it I will.

I awoke six hours later, just before midnight. Despite me asking him not to, I expect to hear from Ollie tomorrow, but I won't be here to answer.

I had prepared a backpack with a few outfits, some supplies, and a duffel with weapons and money, and I left the property in the same way I did when I visited Randallstown the last time. They won't figure out I'm gone until morning, which gives me plenty of time to separate myself from their prying eyes.

I had Mark pick me up and take me to my car. When I told him he'd probably never see me again, we hugged and he said he'd miss me and to be safe.

I'm currently on the road heading south and west, generally, on my way to find the truth of who I really am.

When I was five years old, my parents mysteriously disappeared and were never found. From that day forward, I have been alone in the world. My name is Josey Baldwin. Their names were Darren and Lucy Baldwin. The state placed me at Randallstown Children's Home under the care of Dr. Rosemary Greenburg.

That is the story I've been told and have always believed to be true. As it turns out, my story is a fabrication. My name is made up. My parents, as described to me, were a figment of someone's imagination. The real story of what happened to my parents and how I came to be in Randallstown is still a puzzle I need to solve.

There are secrets out in the ether, secrets with secrets of their own that I need to uncover. Madame K knows the truth behind this whole affair. Her direct involvement in the events surrounding my parent's disappearance but apparent murder, is yet undetermined. When I find out, I intend to rip this shit wide open.

With each passing day, the circle of people I trust is dwindling. One of my greatest concerns about becoming and living in the world of an assassin was the inherent danger and the distrustful nature of the business. My worst expectations keep coming true. Madame K is now my enemy. Ollie has broken my heart and hardened my armor. My team has been destroyed from within. My life has become a mess of epic proportions and I'm mad as hell.

For now, I'm rogue. I don't know what my future with AWT will be. I don't know what the future of the company itself will be. It will remain that way until I uncover the full truth. I have no desire for this, but if it comes right down to it, I will kill to get the answers I want. And since my entire world is collapsing around me and every person I thought was on my side is turning out not to be, I guess I'll just have to be alone, fight alone, and if I have to, kill alone.

Epilogue

2 months later

In the suburb of Agios Dimitrios, Athens, Greece, an abandoned house on the southwest end has been setup to achieve the goal of extracting information by means of torture. It took Amatto less than thirty days to track down Nestor and Sofia Kokinos, the brother and sister that hired AWT to kill Gus Taggert and Denis Koplen. He found it shockingly easy. They had to know they'd be targets. Perhaps the Atlantic Ocean and the international borders gave them a false sense of confidence. Regardless, there was no obstacle big enough to keep them safe once Amatto was given carte blanche to find out what they were digging around for, and eventually, kill them.

With Sofia and Nestor each strapped to a chair, arms tied behind their backs and facing each other, Amatto goes to work on them. Sofia's eyes are filled with tears, her mouth covered in duct tape. Nestor's face is full of dread and uncertainty. He's knows what this little meeting is about though. He's been instructed not to speak unless spoken to.

Amatto starts slow and easy, looking at Nestor, "Okay, this can be really simple or it can be really difficult. The choice is yours. I ask a question, you give me an answer. Each time you don't or if I think you're lying, I hurt her. Nod if you understand."

Nestor nods.

"Just to make sure you know that I'm not fucking around," Amatto turns to face Sophia. Without warning, he lays a vicious backhand to the left side of Sophia's face, nearly knocking her over. Her muffled screams send tears down the face of her brother, who despite wanting to blurt out, holds his tongue.

"Question number one. Did you blackmail Emily into sabotaging the Taggert and Koplen contract?"

"Yes, yes," Nestor answers.

"Good.

"Question number two. We discovered that Emily was attempting to hack into our computer systems. Why? What information were you seeking?"

"We don't know anything about that, I swear," Nestor says.

Amatto pulls a knife from his waist, and with no hesitation, plunges the blade deep into the right leg of Sophia, three inches above the knee. He removes his hand, leaving the knife in place. Amatto understands how quickly she would die if he pulled it out.

Her stifled yelp and whining hide her agony. The pain nearly makes her pass out. Her head slumps, her face red and sweaty.

Nestor cries out, "You son of a bitch! Stop! Stop!"

"You lied. And now you're breaking the rules." Amatto speaks calmly, his heart rate barely escalating. From his right hip, he pulls a .45 caliber pistol from its holster and takes dead aim at Sophia's forehead. Making sure Nestor can see, he brings the barrel of the gun to within two inches of her face.

"Please, please don't!" Nestor is practically spitting the words. "We wanted to get our money back from the contract." He sighs. "She never even got that far. Your systems were impossible. Please don't hurt her anymore. I'm sorry."

Amatto turns and points the gun at Nestor. "You weren't looking for anything else?"

"No, no. We paid a couple million dollars for that contract. We got greedy and figured, hell, if we got her doing this sabotage stuff for us, why couldn't she hack into their bank accounts and get our money back?"

Amatto believes him. "Okay. Be quiet now. I need to think."

He wants to make them suffer for what they did to AWT, the Kill Team, especially to Josey, but he's growing bored of their whining and their faces. And he's tired. He wants a beach somewhere to relax, get laid, have a cocktail. If he ends it right now, he can go and lay low for a while and do exactly those things. For the Kokinos, that means they will never again see the light of day.

Amatto reaches over to Sophia with his left hand and yanks the knife from her leg, wiping the blade on her pants before returning it to its sheath. He then turns to Nestor and puts a bullet through his left eye socket.

Two minutes later, the siblings are gone.

Four hours later, after some clever disposal and cleanup, Amatto is gone too.

KILL TEAM

ABOUT THE AUTHOR

Richard's fifth major release, Kill Team, the second of the Kill Series, continues the story of Josey Baldwin as she traverses the world of contract assassination. His previous works include Kill Academy - Kill Series Book One (2017), RejectGuy99 (2015), A Room Full of Keys (2013), & Neither Snow, Nor Rain, Nor Zombie Infection (2012).

He currently makes his home in Central Illinois with his wife, Amy, and their Cavachon, Padraig. Reading, writing, playing videogames, watching independent films, and DIY projects are among his favorite pastimes. He's been told the cookies he makes from his self-created recipes are worth killing for but he'd rather people not shed blood over them. Everyone can have a cookie. Just chill.